ENTANGLED

BOOK IV

NICOLETTE JOHNSON

Day-N-Night Publishing

ISBN: 979-8-9852137-4-4

Library of Congress Control Number: 2022921102

Cover Photo 2022 www.authornicolettejohnson.com. All rights reserved-used with permission.

Author Photo 2022 InterSeeding Shutters Imagery, LLC. All rights reserved-used with permission.

PRINTED IN THE UNITED STATES OF AMERICA

❀ Created with Vellum

"You never know how strong you are,
until being strong is your only choice."

Bob Marley

PRELUDE

LENNY

TEN YEARS EARLIER

"Nigga, get the fuck up. We got to get the fuck up outta of here." I grab my homeboy's arm and drag him down the lane. Niggas shootin' left 'n right. "We gotta get the fuck up outta here!"

My homeboy was shot in the leg, slowing us down, but I can't leave him, not now. He the only family I got except for my moms.

I knew it was a bad idea to fuck that white broad. What the fuck? Man, White Boi is fucking crazy.

We manage to jump over a fence and land in the backyard of a dilapidated shithole. Grass knee-high and fucking gnats everywhere, eatin' us alive. We crawl under the rundown, tick-infested house and sit until the coast is clear.

"You good, Jay?" I ask my homeboy. We've been friends since diapers. Our moms grew up in Mario Land on the Eastside of Savannah. Ever since, we been thick as thieves.

Jay doesn't respond, so I nudge him again, "Jay, you good?"

He doesn't move.

"Fuck." I roll him over, and his eyes are rolled to the back of his head. "Jay, come on, man. Get up. This shit ain't funny." I shake him harder this time.

I then hear sirens. Fuck, I need to get help. Those niggas are long gone by now. So, I make a split-second decision. I crawl from underneath the house and take off, running around the front and flagging down the cops.

"Over here. Over here," I yell, waving my hands in the air.

A cop pulls up behind me, and I show him where my homeboy is. Then, when the cop turns his back to look under the house, I run and never look back again.

CHAPTER 1

DIANELLA

*J*t's hurricane season, the calm before the storm. The skies are grey, and the breeze is sifting through the cracks. I've been feeling so lost lately and can't get out of this funk. I'm usually the life of the party and full of joy and mischief. But recently, I find myself contemplating my decisions and actions in life.

I decide to get up out of bed and bake a cake amid a storm. Good thing my brother, Jason, installed a backup generator for the café and my loft right above it. It's in the middle of the night, and I glide downstairs to get started.

I have a three-bedroom loft that's perfect for me. Jason had it built with an open concept to give me much-needed space. It's above the café, so I can just roll out of bed if I want to and go to work. It has a rustic feel with brick accent walls in the living area and master bedroom. I love earthy tones, so I have the browns and light blues to give me a serene feeling when I walk into my home. I have a guest room for friends and family and an office to finish my work in the evenings. I live in an up-and-coming neighborhood with plenty of little shops and restaurants. It might not be in the downtown of Savannah, but it's in the heart and soul of Savannah's midtown. They call it the Starland District.

Baking calms me and puts me in a place of peacefulness and hopefulness. In my enormous kitchen, I pull the eggs, cream, and milk from the restaurant size fridge and set everything down on the large stainless steel island. I then grabbed the flour, baking powder, sugar, and room temperature butter.

"I think I'll bake a double fudge chocolate cake." I turn on some music, and I get into my zone. 'I see Red' is playing, and I'm mixing all my ingredients and dancing to the smooth sounds of drums, electric guitar, and strong vocals. I turn on the oven to preheat, ready to make my delectable creation.

My mind drifts to a month ago, when Lenny, my boyfriend, confesses that he was part of a gang on the Eastside of Savannah. I was so upset with him that I just walked away and never looked back. He said he was trying so hard to get out because he wanted a better life, but I still didn't give him the time of day, I couldn't.

He has to understand that I grew up without a mother and a father because of the very thing he committed to doing every day, selling drugs on the streets. My mother was a heroin addict. I don't remember her well, but my brother said she was sensational until our father left us. She went downhill from there. Sometimes I wonder where our father, or better yet, sperm donor lays his head at night. Whatever, pushing that depressing thought out of my head.

Lenny is the epitome of a strong Black man from the Eastside of Savannah. He had to grow up without a father in his life and had to watch his mother work, day, and night, to put food on the table. Thirty percent of Savannah's population is in poverty, and Lenny is part of that statistic. He grew up with nothing, and when the time came for him to help out his mother, he chose a family that caused him so much pain and heartache. A family that commits crime to provide. A family that tortures for fun. A family that takes without asking. Eastside Boyz is what they call themselves. And if you ever cross their path, you will regret being born.

Lenny called them family once, and for the most part, they were at the time. He craved the attention of a father and was desperate to help his mother, doing the very thing his mother would cry at night for him to never do. He became an Eastside Boyz thug.

I was so hurt and so shocked that he could ever be a part of something like that, but then again, how could he not. It's the environment that he was subjected to every day of his life.

I start pouring the mixture into a pan when I hear a knock on the front door. Startled, I look up. "That's weird. It's late at night. No one should be here this late." I grab my phone and walk to the front of the café to see who it is. I see blue lights through the glass window and realize it's a cop. I open the door and see a gorgeous man in uniform standing nice and tall, with skin the color of vanilla ice cream, beautiful grey eyes, and curly brown hair cut short. He has tiny freckles on his cheeks, so small, you would think they're blemishes. Yet, he exhibits confidence and pride in his demeanor. I like that in a man.

I turn the alarm off and unlock the door. I then open it.

"Hi, can I help you?"

"Yes, ma'am. I saw the lights on while patrolling the area and wanted to ensure everything was okay. Unfortunately, there's a storm coming, so the curfew has been activated for the evening hours."

"Oh, I see. I was just baking a cake. I couldn't sleep, and I bake when I can't sleep. I didn't mean to cause alarm." His voice is seductive and smells of sandalwood, spice, and musk. Jesus, he smells so good.

"No, ma'am. Not alarmed; I just know you're normally closed at these hours. This is my area to patrol, so if you need anything, don't hesitate to call."

"Of course. And your name, officer?"

5

"Sergeant Lamonte Wilson."

"Well, it's nice to meet you, Sergeant Wilson. My name is Dianella Hall. I own the café. I will be sure to call if I need anything. And stop by anytime. We definitely support the police."

"Of course, I usually am heading home when everything opens up. Um, by any chance, you aren't related to Jason Hall?"

"Yes, he's, my brother. He's a detective in Homicide."

"Wow, small world. He's a good friend of mine. He always talks about his sister, but it didn't dawn on me until just now that you two are related."

"Yeah, you must be a good friend. He usually doesn't talk about family to just anyone."

"Yeah, he's a private person, but I've known him long enough to see right through his walls."

"Well, that's good to know. But, wait, just a minute. I want to give you something."

"Yes, ma'am."

"Oh, you don't have to call me ma'am. It makes me feel old. Dianella is fine with me." I grab my business card off the counter to give to him.

"Of course, ma—Uh, Dianella."

"Here. This is my business card. Please don't hesitate to ask if you're ever in the area and would like a coffee or pastry."

"Well, Dianella. Do you happen to have coffee now?"

I look into his eyes, and I see curiosity in them. Then, contemplating if I should, but before I know it, I spit out, "Yes, of course. I'll put on a fresh pot." So I let him in and locked the door behind us.

I guide him to the back of the café to the kitchen area. God, I should not be doing this, but there's something about him that's intriguing. I want to know more.

"You can sit here," I offer, pointing to a stool under the island Jason had built for me to work at.

"Thank you." I put a pot of coffee on, then put my cake into the oven and set the timer.

"So, do you always work the night shift or rotate your schedule?" I ask.

"I rotate every month."

"Do you like being on nights or days?" I ask because he seems a little reserved.

"I prefer nights better. During the day, we get a lot of miscellaneous calls, and during the nights, I know I'm working to help someone. And of course, all the brass is not working at nights either," he chuckles to himself. I remember Jason sayin the same thing.

"How long have you been an officer?"

"About ten years now, and I enjoy every bit of it."

"Well, that's good to know. We need more officers like you."

"How about yourself? Have you always wanted to be in the culinary arts?"

"Well, I went to school, originally, for nursing. But over time, I realized my passion is baking and cooking, so I decided to get my license in culinary arts and became a chef."

"Wow, a nurse and a chef. How did the world get so lucky?" I feel my cheeks heat at the compliment and glance away. It's been a long time since I've had someone compliment me on something. Even Lenny hasn't done that in a while. "I didn't mean to make you uncomfortable."

"Oh, no. You didn't. I just—"

"No need to explain." I turn around, look into his eyes and see that he's genuine in his statement.

"It's just complicated."

"Got it. I can leave if that would make you feel more comfortable."

"Oh, no, Sgt. Wilson. Besides, you need your coffee. I'm not going to let you leave without it."

"I appreciate that. And you can call me Lamonte."

"Of course, Lamonte." The coffee stops brewing, and I grab a mug and fill it up. "Would you like cream or sugar?"

"No, just black."

"Coming right up." I hand him his coffee and then pour me a cup. I like mine with sweet cream. "So, are you from Savannah?" Pouring creamer into my coffee.

"Yes, born and raised. My parents live downtown."

"I never met my parents, but Jason and I had a wonderful mother figure. She raised us both on the westside of Savannah."

"Yes, I remember Jason mentioning that once. You guys were adopted, right?"

"Yeah. Big Mama, well, Allison Taylor, took care of us until the day she died. So now, it's just Jason and me."

"Sorry to hear that."

"Don't be. It was a long time ago."

"Dianella, it's been a pleasure, but I don't want to overstay my welcome. Besides, I have some more rounds to make before my shift is over."

"Oh, yes, of course. I didn't mean to keep you."

"No need to apologize. I enjoyed your company. And thanks for the coffee. It really hit the spot."

"My pleasure. Stop by anytime."

"Thank you." He hands me his empty mug and turns to walk to the front door. I feel the urge to keep him there longer, but I force the thought out of my mind. I follow behind him and rush to unlock the door. I turn around, and he's mere inches from my face. I feel heat running across my skin and chills running down my spine. Having him this close to me gives me butterflies in my stomach. I look into his eyes, and I feel a serene desire pulling at the pit of my stomach, my soul. Finally, after what seems like forever, I tear my gaze from his.

"Oh, I'm sorry. Didn't mean to bump into you."

"You really have to stop apologizing," he states matter of factly, stepping back so I can open the door.

"Have a safe night Lamonte."

"You to Dianella. And thanks for the coffee. It was very intriguing." Interesting choice of words, intriguing. And God, I love the way he says my name. He then walks out without saying another word. Shit, that was intense.

I never felt anything like that before. I then hear a beeping sound.

"Shit, my cake." I lock the door behind me and set the alarm. Then, I rush to the kitchen to remove my cake.

"Perfection."

CHAPTER 2

LAMONTE

a sunrise is one of the most glorious moments you can ever experience. Its beauty is a force to be reckoned with, giving me renewed hope every morning of my life. I sit and watch as it rises and gives life to the city. A storm is coming; you would never know it by looking into the open river free from condensation. Every morning, I have the opportunity to witness this eccentric, phenomenal while the earth sleeps and the creatures slither.

This is my favorite moment working the night shift every night of the month. While watching the sun harden the souls of last night, my mind drifts to the most angelic creature of them all, Dianella Hall.

Opening the door stood a five-foot-six beauty with pure milky skin glistening in the moonlight. Her long brown hair draped around her delicate shoulders. When she looked into my eyes, her green emeralds pierced my soul.

I've never witnessed such beauty in my life. It took every ounce of my being to keep my composure. She smelled of cakes and cookies the moment I walked past her.

Jason always talked about his sister, but he never mentioned how hot she was. Fuck, he's going to kill me if I even try to talk to her.

I call in the first half, "Dispatch, can you call in the first half?"

"10-4," announces Dispatch over the portable radio. "All even units, please end your tour of duty."

I walk back to my patrol car and start heading home. I live not too far from the precinct, in the heart of the downtown area. I own a townhouse on Oglethorpe Ave between the fire station and the police department. Very convenient for my family and me.

A little while later, "Dispatch, can you call in the second half and log me off for the night? Have a good morning," I project on the radio.

"10-4." I then turn my radio off, leaving the next shift to handle whatever is thrown their way. It's good to be back on the streets. For the past couple of months, I've been on administrative leave for racially profiling in the downtown area. To be honest, I had no idea I was even doing such a thing, well not until it was brought to my attention. More like, called out on my shit by Bradley. He changed me for the better and now that I know, I hate myself even more. I'm a Black man for Godsake. I should know better.

My mind drifts back to Dianella, and I wonder if I should try to pursue her. I'm pretty sure she must be taken, and I don't want to be that guy, but there's something about her. I don't know how to explain it. I never felt anything like it.

Every girl I've been with has never piqued my interest as much as Dianella did last night, and I haven't even touched her. I really just need a fix and never call back again. It's probably fucked up of me to do that, but I have no desire to pursue something that means nothing to me. But Dianella, on the other hand, definitely captured my attention.

I pull my patrol car into the garage at the back of the house. Here in Savannah, we have lanes to access our driveways. The front of the house has parking, but you have to pay for it through the city. No need to do that when I have a four-car garage. I get out of the car and close the garage. I walk up the stairs to enter my home.

It's not as big as my parents', but it's right for me. Standing at three stories, with an open concept, my living space is on the first floor with a kitchen designed for a chef with stainless steel appliances and an island large enough to accommodate twenty people. The counters are made of black slate, and the island is made of soft grey granite. The cabinets are made of glass to see exactly where everything is.

Walking past the kitchen, you enter the living space furnished with rustic brown seating and rustic accent tables. I have an eighty-four-inch TV on the wall, perpendicular to the living space and the kitchen. I like to watch sports in both areas.

I have three balconies on each floor furnished with outdoor wicker furniture. After grabbing a beer out of the fridge, I head to the second floor, where I have four guest bedrooms fully equipped with a different theme in each room. They all have their own full bathroom as well.

I then make it to the third floor, where my sanctuary starts. I have a gym and an office on this floor. But my most private area is my bedroom. I don't let not one person step foot in this room, except for Connie, my housekeeper. So when I bring girls over, they don't even have the option of a tour of this floor.

It's all mine.

There's a king-size bed on one side of the room and nightstands flanking each side. I have a large walk-in closet on the opposite side of the room and a significantly large bathroom parallel to that. I have both a garden tub and a walk-in shower. I take my duty belt off and hang it on the stand in the closet. I start to strip my uniform, piece by piece, removing my ballistic vest, shirt, and pants.

I then get in the shower and run lukewarm water down my back. My mind drifts back to Dianella, and my dick stands at attention. It's been a while since I've had pussy and thinking about her ain't helping. I try to push her out of my mind, but then I think about those gorgeous green eyes and those sexy ass thighs, and I just lose my mind all over again.

I turn the water to cold to calm the fuck down. After washing my ass, I get out, get dressed in sweats, and head to the kitchen to get another beer. I know it's seven in the morning, but for me, It's seven in the evening. I run back upstairs, drink my beer, and go to sleep. Waiting for my night to start all over again.

CHAPTER 3

DIANELLA

The morning rush at The Grind, my café, gives me adrenaline every time. Well, not mine alone. I own it with my brother, Jason. Some day, I want to buy him out, so I can open more just like it. I love the people coming and going on about their day. Of course, I will rather be in the kitchen baking, but I also enjoy the hustle and bustle of serving the good people of Savannah.

Maggie, my cashier, and server, is a Godsend. She has really stepped up over the months since Amelia decided to run off and get married. Don't get me wrong, Brad is a wonderful guy, and I absolutely love Amelia; I just miss my best friend, sister, and confidant.

Sometimes I feel intrusive when I want to spend time with her, even though she says I'm being ridiculous. Maybe I am.

Jason, my brother, married her sister Lily and had beautiful triplets, two boys, Jacob and Johnathan, and a girl, Jasmine. Amelia married Brad and adopted his daughter, Annabelle. And of course, Ryan, Jason's best friend, married Kim and had a baby boy, Ryan Junior. I think I'm the only one who has not married nor had a kid yet. Thank God. I'm way too busy for that right now. I'm in the prime of my life. Why would I want to change that?

I head to the back to grab some more pastries when I hear someone call my name. I turn around, and it's no other than Lenny Bradford. Annoyed by his presence, I continue to walk towards the back.

He knows not to follow me. I grab the pastries and head back to the front counter.

"Please, Dianella. I need to talk to you. Can you just hear me out?"

"I'm busy, Lenny. I don't have time to talk right now."

"How about later? I'm not leaving until I speak with you."

"Fine, come back around three. The crowd would have died down by then." He flashes his perfect smile, turns on his feet, and walks out before I can change my mind.

"I'm so angry with him right now," I roar, not even realizing it.

"Why is that?" asks Maggie.

"He confessed something to me, and I don't know if I can accept it," startled by her presence. I didn't know anyone was back here.

"Is it that serious?"

"Yep, it's that serious to me."

"Well, like I said before, men come by the dozen. So you have plenty to choose from."

"You're right about that." We then laugh and continue serving the customers.

Boy did the time fly by. It's two-thirty, and the afternoon rush has come to a crawl. I head to the back and let Maggie take care of the front. I usually count the morning profits around this time and prepare them for the drop on Fridays. I have another girl who helps on the weekends while attending school during the weekdays. Christy has been an enormous help to our weekend crowd.

"Dianella, you have a visitor up front." Damnit. I don't feel like dealing with Lenny right now. I put the morning profits up and head to the front. I look up, and it's not Lenny. It's that gorgeous cop from last night, Lamonte. My God, he's sexy as hell. That curly hair and beautiful grey eyes. He looks delicious outside that uniform. He's wearing a white tee that looks like his little brother's shirt and dark blue jeans that hug his ass just right.

Shit.

I approach the counter and realize I probably look like a hot mess. Shit, I feel my cheeks turning into firepits, and I just want to crawl under the counter at this point.

"Good afternoon, Dianella."

"Hi, Lamonte. What a pleasant surprise. Shouldn't you be sleeping right now?"

"I only need a couple of hours, and I'm good to go. I thought I would take you up on your offer." I just stare at him, hypnotized by his voice. "Dianella?"

I feel Maggie hit me on the side, and I wake up out of my trans. "Yes, sorry. What type of pastry would you like?" I'm such a blubbering fool right now.

"What do you recommend?" he smirks a little, showing that cute little dimple on his left cheek.

"My favorite is the éclair with cream and fruit. But they all taste delicious."

"I would hope so; you are the chef." I then laugh out of nowhere. "I will take the éclair and a cup of coffee."

"Sure thing." I grab a clean dish and place his éclair on it with a fork. I then hand it to him and get the coffee. "Black, right?"

"You remembered."

"Gotta know my customers." I pour his coffee and hand it to him. "You can have a seat anywhere."

"Thanks, Dianella," he bows a little and winks at me.

He fucking winked at me.

Holy shit.

"Of course. You're welcome."

He then turns and finds a seat. I head to the back and sink into a weeping mess.

"What the hell was that?" asks Maggie as she strolls to the back to find me wallowing in my misery.

"Nothing."

"The hell it's not. I've never seen you act like that around anyone. Do you like him?"

"No, no. I can't; I have a boyfriend, remember?"

"Yeah, I remember, but do you remember?"

"Shut up, Maggie. He's just a friend of Jason's. They work together."

"Really. He's a cop?"

"Yeah."

"Well, damn. H can handcuff me now and throw away the key. That man right there is sexy as hell, like sex on an ice cream cone dripped with white chocolate."

"Stop it. He will hear you," I seethe through clinched teeth.

"Let him."

I look up and shit. It's Lenny. I forgot all about him. I jump to my feet and walk to the front counter.

"Hey, let's head to the back. We can talk there. Maggie, can you watch the café for a while?"

"Sure. Take your time," Maggie smirks. She's so enjoying my agony.

Lenny then walks behind the counter and tries to kiss me on the cheek, but I back away. I look around him and see Lamonte glancing out the window. Thank goodness. I then turn around and head upstairs. We enter my loft, and I decide to sit in the living room.

"So, what do you want to talk about?"

"For starters, I want you back. I miss being with you."

"You know why I can't right now."

"I know, and I'm trying to fix it."

"How? How do you fix this?"

"I've been trying to get out, but there's only one way."

"And what is that?"

"I can't tell you."

"You can't, or you won't?"

"Both. It's more for your protection than mine."

"Do you see why I can't be around you now? I run a business, have family, and have nieces and nephews around me all the time. I can't put their lives in danger."

"I get it. I understand. I will do what I have to."

"Actually, I think we should take a break. This is a lot to deal with right now," I pull my legs up in my chair. My heart beating uncontrollably.

"Dianella, I will make this right. I promise you."

"Just be careful. I know how people like that can be. It will be tough to just leave."

"I know. I'm trying to figure it out."

"All I ask is for you to do is be careful."

"No need to worry about me. I can take care of myself," flashing that infectious smile.

"Yes. I know." I then get up, and he pulls me back down on his lap and tries to kiss me. I push him hard on the chest and manage to get out of his grip. "What are you doing?"

"I was hoping for a kiss."

"I literally just told you I want a break. I don't want a kiss. So please leave now!" pointing to the door.

"Dianella—"

"Now!" He drops his head in defeat, preparing to leave.

"Dianella, I really miss you."

"Do what you need to, and I will think about it."

"That's all I'm asking." He then walks out of my loft. Letting out much needed breath, I brush myself off and head downstairs to help Maggie with the café. I had no idea I was holding it in.

Walking downstairs cautiously, I see Maggie. "Hey Maggie, did Lenny leave already?"

"Yeah, he left. He looked pitiful and disappointed. Is everything okay?"

"Yeah, we decided to take a break for now. He has some stuff to take care of."

"Oh, I see. By the way, your friend is still here."

"Oh, thank goodness. I was hoping Lamonte would still be here." As I walk over to Lamonte's table, an older good-looking man strides into the café, and I could have sworn it was Jason, but a lot older. I have to do a double-take because the resemblance is incredible.

That's so bizarre.

He steps up to the counter, and Maggie greets and serves him coffee. He then leaves. Crazy, no, it can't be. I've never seen my father.

There's no way he just walks into my café out of the blue. I shake that thought out of my head and continue to head over to Lamonte's table.

He's sitting by the window, with his back to the wall so he can see everything in the café. Must be a cop thing because my brother and Lily always fight over that seat.

"Hey," he looks up at me with those gorgeous grey eyes.

"Hey yourself."

"Sorry about that. I had to take care of some things."

"Oh, it's okay. I know you're working. Would you like to join me? I'm almost done with my coffee, but I don't mind having another."

"Sure. Maggie, can you pour two cups of coffee, one black and the other is for me?" I yell to Maggie.

"Absolutely. Coming right up."

"So, where were we?" I ask.

"Well, you were going to have dinner with me Saturday night," he states matter of factly.

"Oh, I see. I didn't know you asked."

"I'm asking now."

"Where do you want to go?" I ask curiously.

"I would like to cook for the chef. If that's okay with you?"

"You want to cook for me?"

"I prefer an intimate setting, and I think I can show you a thing or two."

"Oh, really? How can I say no to that, someone cooking for me for once? What time should I arrive?"

"Seven, and I'll send you my address."

"Perfect. I must get back to work, but I'll see you on Saturday." I then stand up with my hands in my pocket. I have no idea what to do or say, so I just stand there like an idiot.

Maggie walks up behind me, and I nearly jump out of my skin. "Here's your coffee."

"Oh, God, you scared me. Thanks, Maggie."

"Yes, thank you, ma'am."

"Anytime. Dianella, you can take the rest of the day off if you want. I can take care of things here," Maggie offers.

"Oh, no. I have payroll to do today. Maybe next time, I'll take you up on that offer."

"Okay," she winks, then walks away with an evident smirk on her face. She's such an ass.

I then turn around and nearly bump into Lamonte again. "Shit, I mean shoot. I'm so sorry. I'm very clumsy lately." He grabs me by my arms and steadies me on my feet. I instantly feel a current shoot through my arms and straight to the pit of my stomach. What in the hell was that?

"No, it's my fault. I stood up at the same time you turned around." His voice chills down my spine, and his cologne smell so damn good. I look into his eyes and find myself wanting to fuck him right here, right now. Shit, I need to control myself. I've been so off lately. I pull away, and I feel lost without his touch. That is odd. I wonder if he feels the same thing.

"Well, thank you for saving me a life of embarrassment," I laugh off nervously.

"I will let you get back to work and hope to see you on Saturday."

"Do you want me to bring anything? Like dessert or wine?"

"I got the dinner and wine if you don't mind bringing your special cherry pie. Now, that's my favorite."

"So, you do have a favorite, and to think, I thought you never been here."

"Oh, I've been here. You just never seen me. I usually see Amelia behind the counter."

"Oh, yeah. She's taking care of her bundle of joy these days. I have another girl who helps out on the weekends. Anyways, I will be sure to bring my cherry pie."

"See you then." He then walks around me and out the front door.

I inhale much-needed air and then exhale. Jesus, this guy is going to be the death of me if I keep acting like a freaking raging hormonal schoolgirl around him. I've dated before plenty of times. So why am I acting like this is my first time? Besides, I finally got rid of Lenny, for a while, that is. I just can't be around that stuff. I have too much to lose and to think about. And my entire family are cops. Go figure.

So, what if I go on a little date?

What's the harm in that?

CHAPTER 4

LAMONTE

*S*hit, that feeling again. That electric current running through my veins the moment I touched her. How the fuck does she do that? Seeing her and watching her do what she loves was the best fucking thing to watch. She had flour and cake battery everywhere, but it looked so sexy on her. Dianella is going to be the death of me, and I welcome it with open arms. I never felt anything remotely close to this. Why can't I get her out of my head? Just her demeanor alone is intriguing. She has this meek personality and dares to resolve conflict with restraint.

Hell, I'm just fucking lucky she agreed to have dinner with me. When I saw that guy walk in and head to the back, I knew that was her complication. He looked hopeful when he went up the stairs. He even tried to kiss her. But, when he came back down, he was fucking pissed. She must have broken things off with him. Hell, he's an idiot for letting her go. But, whatever, his loss.

Hurricane Morgan will be here in a few days, and we all pray that it passes right by us. But of course, we still have to prepare for the worse and hope for the best. All of my guys are set either way. Those with kids set up hotels further west for their families, and those without kids or a wife are helping out at the precinct. It's good to have a good group of guys, well, we have one female, Monica Drayton, but you wouldn't know it. She acts just like one of us. Pretty badass when she wants to be.

I decide to call Jason to see how he's doing, well, to be honest, get some information on Dianella and see where he is with me seeing her. I sure hope he's cool with it. So I dial his number, and he picks up on the first ring.

"Hey man, what's up?"

"Nothing, just checking on you and the family. Are you prepared for the storm?"

"As prepared as we going to be. Lily and the kids are staying at Amelia's while I work."

"That's good. I have plenty of room at my house if you need to stay there."

"I think we're good. But thanks for the offer. So, how's life treating you?"

"Well, I'm glad you asked. I think I might be interested in someone."

"Wow… you… interested in someone? Who would have thought?"

"Yeah, man, I didn't think this would ever happen to me, but it's still very new."

"So, what's different about this girl than the others?"

"Well, for starters, she's smart as hell. She has a wonderful personality and always seeks to help others. But, you know how it is; most of the women I date are only after one thing, my money. She's different. But I think she's possibly dating someone."

"I don't know, man, she sounds like a wonderful girl, but if she's seeing someone, you need to be careful. You don't want to mess things up for her and her man."

"That's the thing; I think she called things off, at least I hope she did. She agreed to have dinner with me on Saturday. That's a good sign, right?"

"Maybe, but don't get your hopes up. She may very well end up with the other guy. Just be careful. So, who's this intriguing woman who has piqued your interest? She must be a hell of a woman to do that, especially for you."

"Well, that's the thing, if I tell you, you must be cool, man."

"Now, you've really piqued my interest. Who is she?" he asks cautiously.

"Well, it's Dianella, your sister."

"My what?" he says through clenched teeth. I can hear the rage building through the receiver.

"Just hear me out. I promise you I will not fuck things up with her, and I'll give her the space she needs—"

"My sister, though. Man, what the fuck?" he says, annoyed.

"I know. I didn't know she was your sister until we started talking one night; I was checking on your business. I thought she was one of your employees. I would have never pursued her, but there's something about her. I don't know how to explain it."

"Just stop," he snaps. "Look, I get what you're saying. I had the same feeling about Lily. If you think there's something there and you're not just treating my sister like all the others, then I will give you my blessing, but be careful. She's in a relationship. I'm not a big fan of the guy, but I have to respect my sister's decision even though I disagree with them."

"What's going on with that? He seemed a little pissed earlier today when he left the shop."

"Between you and me, I found out that he's part of a gang. She doesn't know that I know, so keep it like that. My guess she found out and wants nothing to do with him, but that's my assumption.

25

Just don't push her. She'll be honest with you over time. She just tries to handle things on her own."

"Yeah, I get that about her. Hey?"

"Yeah?"

"Thanks for your blessing. I appreciate it. I didn't want to move forward without you knowing."

"I appreciate the mutual respect. And good luck. Oh, and by the way, if you fuck over my sister, I will fuck you up."

"Got it." He then hangs up the phone. That went way better than I thought. He's right about one thing; I can't mess this up.

CHAPTER 5

DIANELLA

*I*t's Saturday morning, and I'm a nervous wreck. I've been making stupid mistakes all morning. Like, one customer asked for a decaf coffee, and I gave him a caramel latte. Another asked for a cream cheese danish, and I gave her a banana nut loaf. After the fourth person, I decided to head to the back and bake a little to calm my nerves.

"Is everything alright with you today? You don't seem like yourself," Christy says, walking back with me.

"I know, right. I'm freaking out."

"What's wrong?"

"I have a date today, and I'm losing my freaking mind. I don't even know why. It's not like I haven't had dates before."

"So, why do you think this date is any different?"

"Every time I'm around him, I become a crazy person. I have no idea why. And to top it off, he's friends with my brother, and I literally just got out of a relationship."

"Wow, you're right. You have a lot going on. First, you obviously like the guy, or you wouldn't be falling all over yourself. Second, if he's friends with your brother, he must be a good guy. Your brother is no one to mess with, and lastly, there's nothing wrong with having fun while thinking things over with your ex. Things will work out if it's meant to be with your ex. If not, then you have options."

"Couldn't have said it better myself," Maggie says, walking in to see what's going on. "Stop panicking over this one date. You never know, he may very well be your future husband, or he could be a psycho no one knows about. Either way, play the field."

"Seriously, Maggie, that's your wisdom?"

"What, I think it's great wisdom and encouragement," she flashes a smile at me, and we all laugh. I really needed this.

"Don't listen to Maggie. Do what's in your heart and stop stressing about what might happen. You deserve to be happy. We all do. By the way, does he have a brother?"

"Uh, I'm not sure. We never got to that point in our conversation. But I'll ask if you want me to," I suggest.

"Absolutely. I need all the help I can get," Christy complains.

"Me too," Maggie chimes in. We all look at each other and burst out laughing.

I hear the bell on the door ring, letting us know someone is at the counter. I look over my shoulder and notice that guy who looks like Jason again. What in the world, two days in a row? What are the odds?

I head to the front counter to help him, leaving Maggie and Christy in the back arguing about relationship advice.

"You know you don't need to find no man. You have a different one every week," Christy argues.

"What I need are better options. Besides, those were all dead beats. I need a real man. A man who can rock my world. All I end up with are little boys who try so damn hard to be men and get nowhere close," Maggie admits while I reach the front counter.

"Hi, what can I get you?" I ask the older guy. He just stands there staring at me like he seen a ghost. "Hi," I announce again. "Can I help you with something?"

"Uh, yes. Sorry about that. I will get a cup of coffee." He continues to stare and makes me a little uncomfortable. His eyes are dark and cold, giving me a serious deadly vibe, which is weird as shit. I don't even know this man. However, he's very pleasant on the eyes for an older man, with short salt and pepper hair, styled perfectly; not one strand astray. He has a long beard covering his chin and dressed in a blazer with jeans. Not bad looking at all.

"Do I know you?" I ask because it's becoming a little creepy now.

Clearing his throat, "Uh, no. You just look like someone I used to know."

"Oh, okay. Here's your coffee. You can sit anywhere. If you need anything else, Maggie or Christy can assist with anything you need." I turn quickly before he says anything else and head to the back. So weird.

Maggie and Christy are still arguing about relationships.

"Seriously, guys. We have a business to run, and if someone could help the older guy up front. He's a little weird, staring at me and stuff. He's giving me bad vibes. In the meantime, I'll be on the lookout for someone for both of you. Now, let me bake in peace, and y'all do what y'all do best," shooing them out of the kitchen area.

Once they leave, I get into my zone. I get my love of baking from Big Mama. She used to bake the most delicious sweets for all the kids in the neighborhood, and I was right there through it all. She was a fantastic cook and baker, and I always wanted to be just like her.

I pull out one of her recipes, homemade cherry pie. Lamonte said this was his favorite dessert, so I must oblige his request. I pull out the flour, fresh cherries, granulated sugar, cornstarch, fresh lemon juice, and eggs. I place all the ingredients on my massive island.

I start with cutting the cherries into halves and pitting each one. Some people would find this tedious, but I find it relaxing and soothing to keep my mind engaged in something meaningful.

A while later, I preheat the oven and then start making the dough for the crust. This was my favorite part of baking. I would toss the flour on the roller pin and roll the dough until it perfectly fits the pan. I love my crust thick, so I would even it out thicker than most pies. I then set it aside and start with the filling. This is the tastiest part; I mix the sugar, fresh cherries, cornstarch, and lemon juice in a large mixing bowl until the cherries are completely coated.

I carefully line my favorite baking pan with the doughy crust so as not to stretch or tear it. Next, I cut the extra dough hanging off the edges for the topping. I then fill the pan with delectable fillings.

Now, to make it look spectacular, I've been creating masterpieces for years, each different in its unique way. First, I roll the extra dough into a slightly thinner crust than the bottom. Next, I carve large and several smaller leaves in different shapes and sizes. I then placed them on top of the pie, creating a colorful glow of reds, golds, vibrant yellows, and earthy browns. It gives an electrifying feel to the mood I'm in right now. Finally, I place the masterpiece in the oven and allow it to mold into transformational magic within the air for this colorful season. Why not create something so perfect for this current atmosphere, hurricanes blazing across the sea, leaves changing, and the trees blending into the landscape with the intention to transform what we all perceive, new growth and new cycles of life.

I feel so much better, so calm and collective. But, I think what I've always wanted to feel is desire.

CHAPTER 6

LAMONTE

The wind has picked up, and the temperature feels excellent without all the humidity. We should have dinner on the balcony tonight. Connie, my go-to person for all my cleaning needs, has done an incredible job setting everything up for me. She offered to cook, but I said no. So it's all on me tonight.

I never learned cooking from my father's side of the family, but my mother can throw down with her good ole southern cooking. Both my parents are from Savannah, born and raised. My mother, Olivia Wilson, is from the Eastside of Savannah. She grew up as a foster child but worked hard to achieve every goal she set for herself. She graduated with honors and started her own company helping children in need. She always said as a Black woman, she had to work harder than the average person; as a foster child, that quadrupled her determination. She met my father, David Wilson, in college. She said she had never met such a charming man in her life. The first time they ever met, she knew he was the one. My father always said the same about my mother. He said what attracted her to him was her beautiful grey eyes and long beautiful hair. He said she was mesmerizing. Because my father is a White man and my mother Black, they had to endure the struggles of the looks and stares of the community, but they never let it bring them down. My father inherited quite a bit of land from his parents, and he just built it from there. He runs the largest construction company in the southeastern area.

I believe my father was hurt when I decided to be a cop instead of helping him run the company, but my mother convinced him that this was something I needed to do. I needed to help others; I think I got that from my mother. Don't get me wrong, I'm damn good with a hammer, but my passion was and still is helping others. The construction thing is my brother's passion.

I walk into the kitchen, trying to decide what I should cook. I think I'm going to cook my mother's famous seafood gumbo. I really hope Dianella likes seafood. Maybe I should text her.

Me: *Hey!*

Dianella: *Hey you. What's up?*

Me: *Do you like seafood?*

Dianella: *Of course. Chef remember…*

Me: *Right, I should have known better.*

Dianella: *It's good to know you are seeking my best interest.*

Me: *Absolutely. By the way, my address is 204 Oglethorpe Ave. Pull in the back; I have a garage in the back of the house.*

Dianella: *Thanks. I will see you soon.*

Me: *Look forward to it.*

Perfect, time to start cooking. I put on some soft jazz and get to work. I want to have at least most of the dish to be complete before I jump in the shower.

I've finished cooking our dinner. I have a nice chardonnay on ice, and the ambiance is set. I changed into something more comfortable, dark blue jeans with a grey button-down shirt. I was told grey brings out my eyes and complexion. We shall see. I hear the doorbell; right on time.

I answer the back door, and before me is the most impeccable creature I've ever seen. She looks even more beautiful when she puts a little effort into her appearance. The wind blows and drifts her hair in the air creating a wave of brown strands splicing the atmosphere. She's standing in heels, bringing her to at least five foot nine. Her beautiful white dress with little green flowers swifts through the wind, causing her to hold it down from lifting up. She looks into my eyes, and I find the most radiant feature on her body. With just a little makeup, she has brightened her eyes to a strikingly green rain forest, ready to set fire to her stage.

"You look amazing."

"You don't look half bad yourself." She stands there waiting patiently for me to let her into my home. Then, realizing what the holdup is, I step back.

"Sorry, please come in." She has the pie in her hand, protecting it from the weather. She walks past me and waits until I close and lock the door. I guide her into the kitchen area. "Welcome to my home."

Once we enter the mud room and walk through the kitchen, she glances around, absorbing the scenery within my living space. "Your home is beautiful. So you're the only one who lives here?"

"Yep. Why do you ask?"

"Well, for one, it's pretty big for only one person. I can fit three of my lofts in your home, and you would still have room," I laugh at her observation.

"I like a spacious environment. I don't feel so claustrophobic."

"Oh, I understand. Where would you like for me to put your pie?"

"Here, I can take it. Dinner is ready whenever you like to eat. I thought sitting on the balcony for dinner would be nice." I hand her a glass of wine.

"That sounds wonderful. What are we having?"

"Seafood gumbo."

"That sounds delicious."

"It's my mother's recipe. She's an amazing cook."

"I sure hope so, or you would be eating TV dinners every night," she laughs, breaking the ice. God, I love her laugh. I love everything about her. I wonder what she feels like. Shit, stop Lamonte.

"Well, if I had to depend on my dad, I would be."

"Tell me more about your family. Have any sisters or brothers?"

"Yes, I have a younger sister, Alexis, and a younger brother, Lemarcus."

"So, you're the oldest?"

"Yep. My brother is about a year younger than me. He works with our dad. My sister is still in college. She hasn't decided what she wants to do yet."

"She will know soon enough. It's good to not have to grow up just yet. Believe me, I know."

"Is it just you and Jason?"

"Yeah, well, not including our extended family," I guide her to my balcony to sit and chat a little before dinner.

"How was it growing up without a mother or father?"

"Uh—"

Realizing her hesitation, I interject, "Oh, I apologize. It's the cop in me. I just meant; that my mother was a foster kid as well. She used to talk about some things, but not all. I could see there were some bad times; she just didn't want to relive it."

"No, it's okay. To be honest, I don't remember a whole lot. It affected Jason more so than me. He remembers everything; I just—I just never wanted to hurt him by bringing it up again. He took our mother's death pretty hard. But, by the grace of God, Big Mama was able to change his perspective of life."

"Wow, I had no idea. I would have never guessed that by the way, Jason carries himself."

"Yeah, he really changed his personality for the better." She takes another sip of wine and starts to glance out over the balcony with an expression of bewilderment yet a calming feel to her demeanor.

"Are you ready for dinner?"

She glances back at me with hope and a smile that will bring light a thousand times. "Absolutely!"

We then get up and walk back into the house. I head straight for the cabinets in the kitchen to prepare the meal while Dianella starts to tour the downstairs living area. She begins with the paintings on the wall.

Each painting tells a story, a story of hopes and desires. A woman standing in a sea of water looking forward to the future and never looking back. A man standing firm in the pits of rubble, desiring to change for the better.

"These paintings are breathtaking."

"Thank you. I find it peaceful to paint what I feel at the moment."

"These are yours?" asked with surprise and astonishment in her voice.

"Yes, I paint in my spare time. It takes my mind off of things and the reality of life."

"You are so talented. Have you shown these to anyone?"

"No, not really. Well, just my parents and siblings. It's just a hobby, not really a career changer for me."

"I beg to differ. You really have a gift."

"Thank you. Dinner is served."

"Perfect. It smells amazing. I'm famished," tearing her gaze from my paintings.

We head back to the balcony and sit at the table under the moonlight, autumn breeze, and soft music playing from the surround sound.

She takes her first bite, and it's like watching soft porn. Her eyes roll to the back of her head, and the soft moaning sounds she makes to amplify the desire I have stewing is driving me insane. How the hell do I stay away from that.

I haven't even touched my food, too busy watching her performance.

"This is the best gumbo I've ever experienced. You must show me your secret."

"No secret at all, but if you keep moaning like that, I won't be able to control myself any longer."

"Who says you need to control yourself?" she deadpans. Holy fuck. Is that an invitation?

"I promised I would be a gentleman. I'm a man who intends on keeping his word."

"Who would know if you broke them other than me?" She takes her spoon into her mouth and swirls it around like a talented lollipop sucker. Jesus Christ, she's undoubtedly prevailing over my willpower.

Clearing my throat, "I would know."

"Well, I guess I won't entice you to break your word. It's honorable to never give up on your promise because your word is all you have at the end of the day." She leaves the subject altogether and continues to eat her dinner.

I promised her brother I would not treat her like any other girl I brought into my life, and I intend on keeping my word on that, but she's making this very difficult, I do say so myself.

She's right about one thing, I put my big toe in this gumbo. My mother would be proud.

"So, what do you do for fun?" I ask her.

"Well, I used to go out all the time, but lately, everyone around me has gotten married and has kids. With me being busy at the café, it's been a while since I've actually gone out. What about yourself? What do you like to do for fun?"

"I'm pretty much a private person. I go away from time to time, but lately, I've had other interests."

"Such as?"

I look intensely into her beautiful green eyes, searching for the correct answer I should say right now. "You."

"Me?" she blushes a little but continues with direct eye contact. This girl does not shy away from a challenge.

"Yes, of course. Why not you?"

"Well, for starters, nothing is exciting about me."

"Why would you say that? I find you very intriguing."

"Seriously? Name one thing."

"Your eyes for starter. There are times when your eyes are the color of jade, like right now, which shows prosperity, resistance, force, and a sense of heroism. But, on the other hand, your eyes present a rain forest, full of adventure and dreaminess, yet melancholy and moodiness simultaneously. Then there's the color of emerald when you are in great thought, wondering and methodically deciding the next path for yourself and others. I find that fascinating and interesting at the same time."

"Wow, I had no idea my eyes said all that."

"A person who pays attention will observe all qualities of who they are interested in."

"So, you're saying you are interested in me?"

"You wouldn't be having dinner with me if I weren't."

"So, you're saying you're interested in every person you have dinner with? I find that hard to believe."

"Only the ones who are granted access to my home and who I take the time to make a special dinner for and who I look forward to, many more to come."

"Well, I probably should be honest about something."

"The floor is yours."

Shifting her gaze from me, "I'm or was in a relationship with someone. He confessed something to me recently that has me questioning my future with him. But the door is not completely closed, and I don't want to lead you on knowing I may have baggage to follow."

"I appreciate the honesty, and I respect your current situation. But, if you ever need someone to take your mind off things, I'm your guy." Jason was right. All she needed was time. I respect honesty from a woman. It's refreshing, to say the least.

"Thank you for being understanding. I, too, am interested in you and find you fascinating; I just can't consciously move into something without closing the other door, even though I want so badly to explore this right here," waving her finger between the two of us.

"Look," sitting forward, so I have her complete attention. "I will wait as long as it will take. There's something here that I want to explore, and I don't usually have interest in anyone. This is new for me, and I'm willing to go as slow or as fast as you want. The ball is in your court."

She puts her fork down and reaches for my hand. The moment she touches me, I feel a spark run down my spine. She flinches a little as if she felt the same thing. I look into her eyes, searching for anything that could explain how I feel in this moment and how she feels.

"I appreciate you, and I'm going to make a promise now. I will not string you along. Please understand that is the last thing I want to do, but I must take care of this situation first, and then I will let you know where I want to go from there."

"That's fair. Now, for dessert," changing the subject before I lose the little control I do have.

"Ah, yes. Dessert. I will get it. You did all the cooking; I can at least serve the dessert."

"Okay," I laugh to myself a little. Never really had anyone offer to serve me in my own house other than Connie and my mother. I can get used to this.

"Sure, but let me help you find everything."

"Oh, please, I'm sure I can find my way around a kitchen. Besides, your cabinets are made of glass. How hard can it be?" she says sarcastically.

"Fine. Be my guest," sitting back down and drinking the rest of my wine, watching her maneuver in my kitchen like a pro. How in the hell did I get so lucky? Well, not lucky yet. She's obviously torn between her complication and me, yet, I still think I have a fighting chance. There's something there, and I will explore it to the bitter end.

"Okay, here we go. Let me know how you like it."

"Wow, are those different color leaves on top?"

"Yeah, every creation I make in my kitchen, I try to put how I feel in that moment, converting the old to make room for the new." And right at that moment, I know I have a fighting chance.

"Well, said. Now, for my favorite part of the night," I take a large bite of her homemade cherry pie, and I fall into a bliss of heaven. This pie right here does it to me every time. "This is amazing. I don't know how you do it but keep doing whatever it is. You will certainly have me as your number one customer."

"Like I always say, I just throw a little dash of love, heart, and soul into every creation I make."

"I can believe it. Eat up, or I will gladly take your share," we both laugh, eating pie and enjoying each other's company.

Never in my life have I ever just wanted to sit and converse with the opposite sex, other than my mother and sister. But I guess there's a first for everything.

CHAPTER 7

DIANELLA

*I*t's early in the morning, and I hear the wind whistling through the cracks and the trees slapping the bricks of my loft. The storm will be here in a couple of hours, and I decided to hunker down and ride it out. We are not getting a direct hit, but Savannah is so old, there's bound to be damage once the storm is over.

I hear my phone ping with a message, and my heart begins to race. Who could be sending me a message this late at night or, better yet, this early? Maybe Lamonte is working tonight. God, I hope not. This weather is going to be pretty bad.

I look at my phone, and it's Lenny. What does he want?

Lenny: *Are you up?*

Me: *I'm responding, so yeah.*

Lenny: *I need your help.*

Me: *Is everything okay? What's wrong?*

Sitting up in my bed, with alert creeping up my spin and worry gripping my nerves.

Lenny: *Can you take me to the hospital? I need help.*

I jump up out of my bed, my alertness on crazy high. Shit, I hope he's okay.

Me: *Where are you?*

After what seemed forever, he drops me his location.

Me: *I'm on my way.*

I run into my closet and throw on a pair of jeans, tennis shoes, and a t-shirt. I grab my phone, keys, and my purse and run downstairs. I turn the alarm off and unlock the door. I then set it again, locked the door, and jumped into my car.

My heart is racing, and I feel myself panicking. I hope he's okay. Please, Lord, be okay. I've been so mean to him lately. I take a deep breath and try to calm myself down a little. I then put the key in the ignition and head to Lenny's location, the Eastside of Savannah.

The rain is really coming down and the wind blowing like crazy. Before I know it, the roads will be flooded. It doesn't take much for the streets in Savannah to flood in this part of town. Make you wonder if the city gives a damn about these people. You don't see all this flooding downtown.

I pull up to Waters Avenue and 37th Street. The last location Lenny dropped to me. To my left, there's a parking lot for an old shopping center. It used to be It's Amazing. It appears that the building is abandoned now. I park and get out of the car. The wind has picked up, and the rain is stinging my skin. I'm soaking wet in a matter of seconds. I can barely see in this weather, but I must find him. I might not want anything to do with his past life right now, but I can't just leave him knowing he needs my help.

I hear something in the corner of the abandoned building near the dumpsters. I cautiously walk over because I have no idea what to expect. I then see Lenny lying on the ground with blood everywhere. His face is unrecognizable, but I know his voice. Even if it's a moan. I rush to his side and drop to my knees.

"Lenny, are you okay? Please, Lenny, get up." I hear him groan loudly like he's in a lot of pain. I decide to run to my car and drive to his location, leaving him for only a moment. I then get out and try to pick him up.

"Jesus, you're so heavy." I put all my strength into my legs and pull him as hard as I can. He screams in pain, but I have to get him into the car. I can barely drag him into the backseat, but I make it happen. Then I get into the front seat and drive as quickly as I can in this horrible weather.

After what seems forever of dodging trees in the road, power lines draping over my car, and nearly hydroplaning, I make it to Savannah Hospital. I pull up to the emergency room and jump out of the car to get some help.

Screaming and begging, "Please, someone help me. I have a man in my car who's badly hurt."

"Yes, ma'am. Get the gurney," the nurse behind the desk calls out to someone.

I then run back to my car and check on Lenny. He has a pulse, but it's very faint. His face has been disfigured, and he's bleeding from the mouth and nose. His legs appear broken, and I can't speak about the internal injuries. "God, I hope he's okay."

Three nurses come rushing out with a gurney, and I help them get him on. "His legs are broken, and he may have some internal injuries."

"What happened?" one of the nurses asked.

"I'm not sure. He sent me a text saying he needed my help. I then found him near a dumpster at an abandoned building at Waters and 37th. I know he was part of a gang trying to get out. This might be the price of him getting out."

"Okay, ma'am. We will take it from here. In the meantime, sit in the waiting room, and we will update you soon."

"Okay, thank you. Oh, by the way, his name is Lenny Bradford," I yell to the nurse, and then I walk over to one of the chairs and sit and wait for God knows how long. "This is all my fault. I pushed him to do this, and now he's suffering because of me." Finally, I pick up the phone and call his mother.

"Hello?" she answers groggily.

"Hi, Mrs. Bradford. I don't mean to call so late, but it's Lenny."

"What is it? What's wrong with my son?" her voice heightens with anticipation and dripping with concern.

"He's in the hospital. We're at Savannah Hospital. He sent me a message saying he needed my help, and when I went to meet him, I —I found him pretty beaten."

"Dianella, I'm on my way."

"Please be careful. The weather is awful and getting worse."

"I will, sweetie. Just hang tight. I'll be there as soon as I can."

"Yes, ma'am."

I then hang up the phone and sit and wait. I find myself crying and breaking down all by myself. The last time I was in this hospital, Bradley, Amelia's husband, was fighting for his life. I seriously hate hospitals. Bad things happen all the time. Subconsciously, I think this is why I no longer want to be a nurse. I've been feeling this way for a long time.

A moment later, I hear someone call out to me. "Dianella?" I look up, and it's Lamonte. "Are you okay?"

"Yeah, it's Lenny. He—," I start breaking down all over again. When will it ever stop? When will lousy shit stop happening to my family?

"It's okay. Take your time," he wraps his strong arms around me and just holds me while I cry. I then hear him talking to someone else. "The victim is in the trauma room. Check on him, and I will stay out here with her."

"10-4 Sarge," the young officer answers.

I gather myself slowly, and he hands me a tissue to wipe my face.

"Are you able to tell me what happened?"

"Yeah, but I don't know much," I confess.

"Just tell me what you do know."

"Okay. I was lying in bed listening to the storm coming in when I heard my phone ping with a message. It was from Lenny." I then grab my phone and show Lamonte the text messages. "He said he needed help and needed me to pick him up. I was scared, so I dropped everything and rushed to the location he dropped to me. I then found him near a dumpster at Waters and 37th. I then used all of my strength to get him into my car and drove him here."

"Why didn't you call for help?"

"I didn't think to at the time. I knew he was losing a lot of blood, and I had to get him to the hospital quick."

"Okay. I understand. Did you notice anything else?" he asks.

"No, I wasn't really paying attention. Everything was happening so fast. It was pouring, and all I could think about was getting him here. I pray I'm not too late."

"Dianella, Jesus, are you okay?" Jason calls out, rushing towards me.

"Yes, I'm okay. It's Lenny."

"You got blood all over you, and you're soaking wet. Are you sure you're okay?"

"Um, yes. It's Lenny's," I repeat, looking down at myself and realize how bad I look. "I called his mother. She said she's on her way. Is it okay if I wait here? I want to make sure he's okay before I leave."

"Yes, of course, but you will need to find a ride back home. We have to take your car for evidence," says Lamonte.

"Really?"

"Yes, sis. It's part of protocol. Lily, Amelia, and Kim are on their way. One of us will take you home. You can use one of our cars until then."

"Shit, you told everyone?"

"Of course. Once I heard your name over the radio, I came straight here. I was on my way home when the call came out. Lamonte, here assured me he would look after you until I got here."

I look up at Lamonte, and I think I see concern in his eyes, but he remains professional. "Is that true?"

"Yes, of course, you're my best friend's sister. We look out for each other." I then see Jason and Lamonte exchange a look like they know something.

"What is it?"

"Nothing, we're going to secure the scene and wait until his mother gets here to brief her on everything," Jason offers.

"Oh, okay." I subconsciously lean on Lamonte's shoulder and wait for Mrs. Bradford to get here. The weather is terrible. I just hope she's careful along the way.

What seemed like forever was only a few minutes when Mrs. Bradford comes running to my side. I must have dozed off because she startles me.

"Dianella, where's my boy?" she yells at me.

Lamonte then stands up and looks into my eyes. I see the sorrow in the midst of worry. He grabs Mrs. Bradford's hands and begins the speech no one ever wants to hear. I drift away solemnly, not understanding why or how I got here.

I hear in the distance, "Mrs. Bradford, I'm sorry to inform you. Unfortunately, your son, Lenny, has succumbed to his injuries. He's no longer with us," Lamonte says, but not in his usual voice.

I hear screaming in the far distance and crying surrounding me, but I don't know why. I slowly stand to my feet, then drift away over a cliff and into the ocean. I feel free and a blissful moment in life where I feel no pain. I see in the distance a woman who looks just like me, smiling and reaching out to me. I then see Big Mama, who has tears of joy running down her face.

"My darling, it's time for you to wake up. You must be by your true love's side and know no matter what, we will be here to guide you through life," Big Mama promises.

"I don't want to go. I want to stay here with you. Can I stay here with you, Big Mama?" I beg.

"I wish you could suga, but you have more to give."

I hear someone calling my name, but I don't want to leave Big Mama.

"You must go, child, and remember we love you and your brother."

My eyes flutter open and see the most exquisite human being standing over me. His eyes remind me of a misty day full of grey clouds surrounding the earth. His curly hair is thrown every which way, probably from constantly shoving his hands through it. He has a five o'clock shadow, which looks good on him. His light blue shirt reflects in his eyes, bringing a serene feel to his gaze.

"Lamonte?"

"Hey, sweetheart. You gave us a scare. How do you feel?"

"I'm fine. My head hurts a little. Where am I?"

"You are in the hospital. Do you remember anything?"

"No, not really…well, let me think." I start thinking of everything that could have happened, and then it just floods back like a tsunami evading a small island.

"Oh, no. Lenny. I have to see him." I try to get out of bed, but my head starts to get really light.

"Hold on, take it easy. You can't see Lenny."

"Please, I have to," I beg.

"I'm afraid you can't. Lenny—"

"Don't. Don't you say it," I spit out between gapping sobs and piercing cries.

"Okay, I won't. But you must get some rest. Promise me you will get some rest."

I turn away from him and stare out the window. It wasn't a dream. It was all true, and it's all my fault.

"Dianella?"

"I promise."

CHAPTER 8

LAMONTE

he pain I saw in Dianella's eyes was indescribable. She's hurting right now, and there's nothing I can do about it. She pushed me away the second she started to remember everything that happened that night.

I've seen people shut down and break down plenty of times in my line of work, but I've never experienced someone close to me go through that type of pain. She won't talk to me; she won't let me help her. I don't know what to do other than to give her space. I just pray she doesn't blame herself because this is not her fault.

Lenny chose that life, and even though he was trying to do right by her, he knew exactly what it would take to get out of a gang. And now that he's dead, they will go after something precious to him, his mother or, God forbid, Dianella.

Jason and I have decided to do around-the-clock patrolling for Mrs. Bradford and Dianella. She doesn't know I'm the one watching out for her loft every night, and I want to keep it that way. I made Jason promise me to say nothing to her.

I know we only had the one date, but it's something about this girl that's different from anything I've ever experienced. She has taken my breath away and never gave it back.

I'm sitting in my patrol car across the street from her café/loft in the middle of the night. The storm has passed by and left minimum damage to the city. I decided to approve some reports when I see the light come on downstairs. I prepare to get out, and then I remember she said she likes to bake when she can't sleep. God, I wish I could see her beautiful face again; look into her gorgeous eyes, and ask her just one more time to have dinner with me.

"Would it hurt to just get a closer look and ensure everything is okay?" Nah, it won't. I convince myself.

I get out of my car and walk across the street. I then see the light shut off, but I hear something in the back. I slowly walk around and find her standing in the lane staring at nothing. She seems so lost, so hurt, so defeated. I decide to walk toward her, clearing my throat, so I don't scare the hell out of her.

"Dianella?"

She turns around quickly, like she never even heard me approach. "Lamonte, is that you?"

"Yes. I was patrolling the area and heard something back here, so I decided to check." Not a complete lie.

"Oh. I was—well, I'm not sure what I was doing. I just can't sleep."

"Don't you usually bake when you can't sleep?" She looks at me like she's surprised, I remember.

"Yeah, but I just don't feel up to it."

"What if I helped you?" She looks up at me again like she wants to say no, but then again, she really doesn't want to be alone.

"Okay, but only if we make something you like."

"Deal."

She pauses for a moment trying to figure out what just happened. She then turns around and walks towards the back door. She looks over her shoulder with those beautiful green eyes and long pretty hair draping her soft skin. She's wearing a thin tank top and shorts so short; it should be a crime to even sell them. But God, does she look amazing.

"Are you coming?"

"Uh, yeah," I clear my throat and follow her. Her kitchen is always so spotless. Unfortunately, some restaurants I enter are nowhere near as clean as her kitchen.

"So, what do you want to make?"

"I really like the cherry pie you make; can you show me how to make it?"

"You want cherry pie again?"

"What can I say? I'm hooked," I shrugged my shoulders.

"I see. Cherry pie it is." I watch her pull all her ingredients out and lay them on the incredibly large island. She then preheats the oven. She grabs two aprons, tosses one to me, then puts on the other. She stands at the counter, putting her hair into a messy bun. She stares at the ingredients, and something just clicks.

Before my very eyes, I watch her turn into someone who has a passion for creating something so delicious. She's moving methodically in her zone, and I just stand there and watch, gapping at every move. It's almost watching a woman dance across the room, and she's the star of the show, and you can't possibly tear your eyes from her. She's mixing, and she's pouring, and then suddenly, she starts to cry, stopping dead in her tracks, slithering to the floor with so much grief in every move.

Taking my duty belt off, I walk over to her and get down on the floor beside her. I lift her up, place her in my lap, and just hold her. In the past two weeks, she hasn't grieved the passing of Lenny. I let her let it all out. "That's it, baby girl. Let it out." I continue to rock her in my arms.

"It was my fault. He would still be here if I never broke up with him. He was so determined to make me happy that he sacrificed himself for me. I never thought in a million years they would hurt him like that. He said it would be okay. He said he could handle it. Why on earth was I so stupid? I should have known that it wouldn't be okay," venting, crying, and yelling between words.

"Look at me." She keeps her head tucked into my shoulder. "Dianella, look at me." I then adjust her in my lap and lift her chin with my free hand forcing her to look into my eyes. "I know that I don't know you very well and that we only had one date, but I must say this. You are not to blame. You told Lenny how you felt and that in order for you to feel safe, he had to change his past and present to be your future. Do not blame yourself for wanting more out of a relationship. For wanting to feel safe, to be able to trust the person, you are with. You are not alone. Every person in this world wants just that and deserves just that. He knew that this would turn out bad; he just didn't know he would lose his life. Dianella, I can tell this man loved you because he respected you enough to get out to try to keep you safe. This is not your fault, and this is not his fault. I see children joining gangs all too often to feel like they are needed and wanted by something. He joined because he knew he needed protection for himself, and his mother and the brotherhood would protect them no matter what. And with that being said, I must tell you something, and you're not going to like it."

Her interest piques, and she listens with wide eyes. "What is it?"

"This isn't over. Because Lenny died, the brotherhood will want something in return. Most gangs beat you until you wish you were dead and leave you be, but not this gang. After he is beaten to death, they will want one more thing to settle his debt. They're going to want someone close to him. That means they will come after you or his mother." She visibly tenses up, and I can sense fear in her demeanor.

"We did nothing to them. I didn't even know until a couple of months ago. I decided to break things off when I found out."

"I know and understand all of that, but they don't care. They will find a way to get to you or her, and when they do, it will not be pleasant."

"I—I can't live like this. I can't be on the run. I have a business. Oh my gosh, my family. My nieces and nephews. Shit, this is why I broke up with him. I can't let anything happen to them. I just can't," slamming her tiny fist into my chest, not feeling a thing because of my vest.

"Dianella, we will not let anything happen to you. I have an idea, but I won't push on the matter. I will only throw it out there as a choice."

"What? What can I do?"

"You can stay with me. I can take a leave of absence and protect you. This will keep you safe and your family safe."

"I can't let you—"

"You're not letting me do anything," I interject. "I'm offering. I know we don't know each other that well, but I feel compelled to be there for you. No matter what."

"What about The Grind, my café? I just can't leave it. I'm the main baker."

"You can still come to work. I will come with you until the threat is over, or I can hire someone to be with you. Whatever and however, we will make this work."

"What about my family?"

"I've already talked to Jason. He agrees that someone needs to watch over you. He said he would do it, but he also has Lily and the kids to think about."

"Yes, of course. I would never jeopardize him, Lily, and the kids."

"So, what do you say?" She looks apprehensive, but she's contemplating the idea.

"I just don't want to put you out or anything. You don't owe me anything."

"I know I don't; however, I want to help, and this is the best solution. They will come here looking for you. They will not know you're staying with me."

"Okay, but you must go about your life like I'm not even there. I don't want you to give your whole life for me. I promise to stay out of the way and —"

"Stop, you're my guest. I will not treat you like a freeloader. Whatever is mine is yours while you are staying under my roof."

She looks into my eyes with fear, hope, despair, and uncertainty. She's scared shitless out of her mind, and I don't blame her. She has no idea what she's getting herself into, and the only hope she has is a guy she barely knows. What's not to fear. But I see this as an opportunity to get to know this remarkable creature.

CHAPTER 9

DIANELLA

*E*ven though the storm has passed, and the nightmare seems to be over, I still feel lost, an unbearable feeling that will not go away. It's raining outside, and the sky is the color of Lamonte's eyes, grey and gloomy, yet hopeful and renowned.

Lamonte gave me an option that I could not refuse. Yet, I still feel uneasy putting his life in danger as well. Even though he brought the suggestion up, I still feel like I can't ask him to put his life on the line to protect mine. Granted, that's what he does for a living, but I can't.

It's wrong.

Sitting on my bed, with clothes scattered everywhere, I'm still contemplating if I should go through with this. So, I do the only thing that comes to mind. I call Amelia.

The phone rings after what seemed forever. Then she picks up.

"Hey, Dianella, what's up? How are you feeling? Are you okay?" Flooding me with dozens of questions.

"Yes, I'm okay. Can you talk for a little?" I ask.

"Of course. What's up?"

"Well, where the hell to start?"

"That bad, huh? How about the beginning?"

"Lamonte offered to allow me to stay at his house because the gang Lenny was with may come after his mother and me. I think it's a bad idea because I don't want to put his life in danger, but I don't know what to do. I'm so scared and confused."

"Wow, that's a lot," I hear Annabelle playing in the background.

"Tell me about it. Are you sure I'm not bothering you?"

"No, no. Annabelle is playing with her toys. She's perfectly fine. And, you called me to get my opinion, so I'm going to give it. Are you scared that Lamonte may do something to you, and that is why you don't want to stay, or is it because you are falling for him and you're ashamed because your recent ex-boyfriend was just killed? You feel like you're betraying him?"

Holy shit, to put it bluntly, she's good. "Well, a little bit of both. I barely know him. I don't just sleep with people, let alone live with them. And then again, I want so much to sleep with him, and I'm scared that I'm hurting Lenny in a way. I feel like I'm cheating on him or whatever."

"Sweetie, you cannot live your whole life thinking that you will be dishonoring Lenny if you start feeling something for someone else."

"But—"

"No buts, put it this way. You were seeing Lamonte before Lenny was killed, right?"

"Yes, but—"

"And you broke things off because you couldn't handle the life he chose to live when he was younger, correct?"

"Yeah."

"Then why are you beating yourself up for something you were going to do when he was alive anyway? Look, you will never forget

Lenny. No one will expect you to, but you can't hold on to something that would have ended in the first place. Lenny should have gotten out for him, not you. He should have done this a long time ago. You cannot blame yourself for his actions. I won't let you. And as for Lamonte, girl, go get your man. I hear he's fine, smart, and rich. He's basically on your level. That's truly hard to find these days."

"I know. Hold on, what do you mean he's rich?"

"You didn't know. Well, I will let you ask him. He has quite a history, from what Bradley tells me. Bradley said he racially profiled him once, but they talked about it, and he changed how he does his job now."

"Wow, I had no idea."

"Yeah, Bradley was upset initially, but they became good friends once he realized he wasn't like that outside of uniform. But he made it very clear he needed to change his ways when he puts that badge on."

"Amelia, thanks for talking with me. You made me feel a lot better."

"Anytime. We must have a girl's night again."

"Yeah, once I settle down, I will call."

"Okay, sweetie, and remember, you are a strong independent woman who can accept help every once in a while, okay?"

"Okay. Love you."

"Love you too."

We then hang up the phone, and I turn to continue packing. I have a lot of stuff, but hopefully, I'm not there for very long.

I'm all packed and waiting for Lamonte to pick me up. I still don't have my car, but then again, I don't want it back. I will never be able to erase the image of Lenny in the backseat bleeding to death.

I shake my head like that's really going to stop me from having to relive that horrific night over and over again. I hear my doorbell, and I nearly jump out of my skin. Shit, I have to calm down. I can't be jumpy for the rest of my life. I grab my bags, lock the door to my loft and head downstairs to the back door where Lamonte is waiting for me.

I open the door, and right before my eyes stands a handsome man full of strength and support. Something I truly need right now. He takes my bags and tosses them over his shoulder like they weigh nothing.

"Ready?"

"Not really, but whatever," I say nonchalantly.

"Don't worry, I won't bite."

"I hope not." He then chuckles and opens the door to his Mercedes-Maybach Exelero, black in color with peanut butter interior.

"Holy shit. This is your car?" I ask with astonishment.

"Uh, yes. One of them."

"Do you know what the hell you're driving? It has a twin-turbo V-12 engine producing 690 horsepower. The top speed is listed at 218 miles per hour. The cost alone is out of this world. Mercedes built the Exelero on the bones of a Maybach. This is insane."

"Yeah, I know. What can I say? I love cars."

"Are you serious right now? People kill for this type of car, and you're just driving it with no care in the world."

"Are you going to get in, or will you just stand there gawking and talking shit about my car?"

"I—I think I'm just going to stand here. There is no way little old me is getting into something like that."

"Well, if you want a ride, you're going to have to get in."

I look at him, and then I look at the car again. How fucking rich is this guy? I might be worth millions, but this car got me beat. He must be worth way more than me. I get in the vehicle cautiously, not wanting to mess anything up or break anything. He then closes the door for me and jogs around to the driver's side. He gets in with a bit of pep in his step.

"You have way too much energy."

"Do I?" he asks with a smirk on his face.

He starts the engine, and I can feel the vibration in my soul. I close my eyes and absorb the feeling of freedom. Jason always had me watching those damn car shows. That's why I know so much about them. I just was never into getting expensive cars. I just need something to get me from A to B and occasionally C.

He pulls off and heads toward his three-story home. The only one on the block. I should have known then that he was filthy rich. I just don't judge people because I don't want them to judge me.

We pull up in his garage, and there are two more vehicles plus his patrol car. Ryan, Kim's husband, is filthy rich, but you wouldn't know it if you passed him on the street. I'm beginning to think Lamonte is the same way.

He parks the car and grabs my bags, and I follow him into his home. I've only been in the living area, the kitchen, and the balcony. I never went upstairs. So, I guess I will get the grand tour now.

"Your bedroom will be on the second floor."

"Where will you sleep?"

"My bedroom is on the third floor."

"Oh, okay. Please lead the way." I'm glad he's trying to respect my privacy. In a way, I want to be alone, just a moment to breathe, to figure out what the hell is going on. Maybe I should ask Lamonte. He seems to know more than I thought.

I follow behind him, not really interested in the tour. I just want a hot bath and lay in the bed.

"Here we are. The room has its own bathroom and walk-in closet. I've had Connie, my housekeeper, stock the bathroom with wash-cloths and towels. If you need anything else, please let me know. Oh, and I normally eat dinner around six. Connie is a great cook if you would like to join me."

"Lamonte," I turn and look up at him before he walks out. "Thank you." He flashes me that beautiful smile, and for a moment, I forget why I'm so, I don't know, so out of sorts.

"You're welcome," he then walks out, closing the door behind him.

I walk around the room, looking at my living quarters as they say in the olden days. The room is absolutely gorgeous and very spacious. It has a beautiful king-size bed with a rustic grey upholstered style. The wall behind the bed has beautiful wooden planks with different shades of light greys and blues. The bed is flanked by white rustic hand-carved nightstands and a matching dresser. The rest of the room is painted a Carolina blue, soft and serene. I then notice that the bedroom has French doors leading outside. I walk over, and it's a balcony with linen curtains for privacy and beautiful lounge furni-ture. It also has a fountain on the side built into the wall. This might be my favorite spot in the whole house. I then walk into the bath-room, and I am blown away.

It's like being in an oasis filled with tropical plants and soothing rain-forest sounds. The bathtub is separate from the shower; from the looks of it, it has at least six shower heads. My gosh, this might just trump the balcony. How in the world does one person live in such a beautiful home all by himself?

What's wrong with him?

I head back into the bedroom and start unpacking my stuff. I put all my clothes in the huge walk-in closet and my undies in the dresser. Man, I wish I had a glass of wine, and then I realize it's almost dinner time.

I walk to my bedroom door and take a deep breath before I walk out. "Here goes nothing." I walk down the hallway and head downstairs. I hear laughter, and then I smell something so savory cooking. My stomach instantly growls, and I realize I haven't eaten in a while, like a couple of days. How am I even functioning right now?

I reach the bottom of the stairs and see a middle-aged Black woman in the kitchen who looks really good, hair softly curled down her back, a pair of jeans with a blouse to complement her aura. She's cooking while Lamonte sits at the island, cutting up veggies. She turns around, grabs everything he cuts up, and puts it in the pan. Lamonte then gets up and gets a bottle of wine out of the wine cellar he has next to the fridge. I continue to walk when Lamonte looks up and sees me walking towards the kitchen area.

"Hey."

"Hi, what's that? It smells amazing," I ask.

"Stewed Okra over a bed of rice and fried pork chops."

"Oh my gosh. I haven't had southern cooking like that since Big Mama."

"Well, I hope you brought your appetite because she made enough to feed an army."

"I'm pretty sure I have. I don't think I've eaten anything in a while."

With concern in his voice, "What's a while?" he asks.

Not wanting to lie to him, "Um, not sure, a couple of days."

"Well, here. Have a seat. You will not go another moment without eating. You have to keep your strength up. By the way, Lamonte here is being very rude. I'm Connie. I'm here for whatever you need," Connie offers.

"Oh, my bad. I just—" Lamonte begins to apologize.

"It's okay, Lamonte. It's nice to meet you, Ms. Connie. Thank you for the lovely meal."

"Of course, honey, and if there's anything you would like, please let me know. I head to the store at least four times a week."

"I do have one request."

"Anything."

"Can I come with you? I sometimes like to go to the fresh market to get all my fresh fruit for my pastries. Baking helps me calm down."

"Absolutely—"

"Actually, I'm afraid that can't happen," Lamonte interjects. "Not right now, at least." I look at Lamonte, and I don't know what to say; I'm speechless.

"It's okay, honey. Give me a list, and I'll be sure to get everything you need," Connie offers.

"So, I can't even go to the Farmer's Market or the store?" shaking my head and ignoring Mrs. Connie's kind gesture. "I can't live like this. I must be free to do what I want when I want."

"I get it. But you have some bad people after you, and the safest place right now is here. If you want to go anywhere, I will have to accompany you. I know this isn't ideal, but it's the best option for now."

I put my head in my hands because I feel overwhelmed with despair. There is no hope for me. How did I get here?

I feel arms wrap around me, and I immediately feel that electricity running through my body again, and it almost feels like a warm blanket soothing my heart, my soul, and I never want to move from this spot.

Lamonte lifts me up from out of the chair and carries me to what I think is the living area. He then sits down with me cradling in his lap. He rocks me back and forth, reassuring me that everything will be okay.

I feel hot tears running down my face, and I just feel lost. I'm so much stronger than this, but for some reason, I just can't take this type of pain, fear, and unbearable grief.

"Why me? Why is this happening to me? When will I get a break? When will I find happiness and a world without heartache and loss? When?" I whisper more to myself than to anyone else.

"You're doing it right now. You're striving for happiness as we speak, and I will be here along the way to help you. No matter what. You will have me here by your side."

"Why? You don't even know me."

"Oh, I know you. I know you're a strong independent woman who strives for pure excellence. I know you've worked hard all your life and don't mind helping anyone. I know you have a heart of gold, yet, you love to have fun. Your passion for baking alone is mesmerizing. You could have said no to my offer, but you didn't. That was the bravest thing you could have done is to accept help from someone you hardly know. That doesn't make you weak. On the contrary, it makes you smart and brave. So, never doubt your worth or your strength. You have suffered a lot, and you're doing remarkably well. I cannot say that about a lot of people."

"How do you do that?" I look up into his gorgeous eyes.

"How do I do what?"

"Calm me down so well, even in the midst of everything I'm going through. I don't know how you do that."

"I don't either. I know that you deserve to be happy, and I want to ensure you get what you deserve."

"And why are you single?" he chuckles a little, almost like a nervous chuckle.

"Well, I haven't found anyone who has sparked my interest. Well, not until you, that is."

"I—I don't know what to say?" avoiding his stare.

"You don't have to say anything. I know it's too soon; just know I'm willing to wait."

"Dinner is served," Connie announces.

"Shit, I mean shoot. I'm so sorry. I didn't realize you were still in the room," I apologize.

"Dianella, it's okay. Connie is not easily offended. Isn't that right, Connie?" Lamonte yells over his shoulder.

"Correct. I've seen everything and heard everything. Besides, I've been around this one long enough to see all kinds of stuff."

"Really, Connie, you're going to bust me out like that?" We all burst out laughing. A laugh I haven't had in a long time.

Lamonte lifts me up and steadies me on my feet. We then walk over to the island, where Connie has set the table for two.

"Are you not joining us?" I ask Connie.

"No, not tonight. I have a date with bingo."

"You play bingo?"

"Every Friday night."

"Don't let her fool you. She's the champion of Bingo Night," Lamonte announces proudly.

"My foster mother loved bingo when I was growing up. I think it gave her peace and a chance to get away from my brother and me. We could be a handful," I laugh at the memory.

"Well, Johnny has been trying to knock me off my throne. That ain't happening by a long shot. Anywho, eat up, and there's dessert in the fridge if you want some. I will see you kids in the morning."

"Okay, Connie. Enjoy your night. We got it from here," Lamonte announces.

"Thank you, Connie. I—I don't know what to say. This is very kind of you," I say.

"Suga, it's my job. I'm here for whatever you want and need."

"Still, thank you."

She looks at me with motherly affection. "Suga, you're welcome." She then turns and walks out towards the door. "Call if you need anything."

"We will, Connie," Lamonte answers.

She then walks out the door. "She's so nice. How long has she been with you?"

"All my life. She used to work for my parents, basically raising me since birth. When I moved out, she came with me. Said, I could never survive without her. She's probably right," he chuckles to himself.

"It's nice to have that type of support. I miss Big Mama every day, so cherish these moments," I feel a tear fall.

"Yeah, I do. Don't get me wrong, my parents have been a huge part of my life, but while they worked or went to different functions, Connie was that mother figure for me."

"Do your parents still live in Savannah?" I ask.

"Yeah, they're just out of town right now." I take a bite of the delicious food Connie made, which is so good.

"Oh my goodness. This food is amazing. It reminds me of Big Mama's cooking."

"I told you. Connie is an amazing cook. Between your café and her cooking, I'll be fat. Good thing I have my own gym."

"You have your own gym?" I ask, choking on my food.

"Uh, yeah. I work a lot of nights, so to avoid working out late at night when I'm off, I had one built on the third floor."

"I guess that makes sense. It's nothing like having your own, and I can only imagine having to adjust your body to be on a certain regimen."

"Yeah, I tried it for a while, and then one day decided to invest in my own equipment. Don't have to wait on someone to finish. Don't have to worry about staph infection. Don't have to worry about whether the gym is closed or not. It's actually nice to have your own." He takes another bite of his pork chop and a sip of his wine to wash it down.

"I can see that. But, unfortunately, I don't have time to work out. So between the café, culinary school, and nursing school, I'm pretty wiped out by the end of the day," I admit shamefully.

"Well, I can't tell. You look great." I feel myself blush from the compliment. He's full of them lately. But I still can't fall for it. I can't betray Lenny like that. Speaking of Lenny.

"Is it okay if I visit Mrs. Bradford? I just feel like I've abandoned her in her time of need."

"I don't think that's a good idea."

"Oh, come on," I drop my fork on the plate, crashing with a loud sound. "I will not be a prisoner of this gang. I want to pay my respects," I demand.

"I can't allow it. It's too dangerous. You can always call but keep the conversations at a minimum. You don't know who's listening."

"Seriously, tell me what's going on. You're keeping something from me. Why are these people so dangerous?"

"Okay fine. I will tell you what's happening, but you have to promise this conversation stays between you and me." I remain quiet, waiting for him to continue. "Promise me." He demands.

"Okay, yes. I promise. I will not tell anyone."

"Good." He then proceeds with the dreadful story. "Eastside Boyz is the gang Lenny was a part of. They are not like other gangs in the city. These thugs don't give two shits about anyone or anything. They will kill and ask questions later. We've tried to shut down that whole operation for years but could never get close enough. So, when Lenny was killed, significant evidence in his apartment may lead us to the gang's leader. They call him the White Hallucination. Your brother and Detective Knight are running the leads now."

"I get that they are killers, but what makes you think they are after me?"

"Well, I was patrolling around your café about a week ago and saw an envelope hanging from your door. It didn't have a return address, so I took it. I know that's wrong, but I had a gut feeling that something wasn't right. It was a message to you, and I intercepted it."

Waiting for him to continue, "Well, what did it say?" I ask impatiently.

"Count your days. We coming for you, bitch." I feel the blood drain from my body and pool into my toes. Then, I see stars, and the room begins to spin.

"What?" I ask myself faintly. I feel my body get really hot, and I can no longer function. All I see is blackness, and I hear ringing in my ears.

I drift into darkness full of fear and unwanted feelings seeping through my pores. Then, the unbearable pain sucks me into a field of isolation and silence. I feel tears run down my face, and I'm no longer in the presence of Lamonte but in the presence of evil.

"Wake up, Dianella. Come on, Dianella, you need to wake up. Face your fears head-on. Have the strength to persevere. You can do this," I hear someone whispering in my ear. "Wake up, Dianella."

I begin to flutter, my eyes open. My soul begins to speak, and my fears begin to drift away. The touch of a warrior brings me to life.

"Here, let me take you to your room. I think you've had enough for tonight." Lamonte, once again, picks me up and carries me to the second floor in his strong arms. I don't say anything because I'm exhausted from everything. He enters my quarters and places me on the bed. He then drapes the covers over me and sits in the chair next to the balcony door. I don't have the strength to tell him I'm okay because I'm not okay. I'm physically and mentally drained from anguish. Before drifting to sleep, I ask myself one last time, why me?

CHAPTER 10

LAMONTE

*I*t's been three days, and Dianella has not come out of her room. Connie has been delivering her food to her room. She can't sit in that room like this. She must get out. I can't let her drift further and further into depression. I have to do something, anything.

I'm sitting in my study trying to come up with some kind of idea to get Dianella out of bed. Then it hits me. She loves baking. I pick up the phone and call Connie.

"Hello Lamonte, what can I do for you?" she asks.

"It's not for me; it's for Dianella. I'm trying to figure out a way to get her out of the room, and it just dawned on me. She loves baking. Can you pick up a few items from the market? I'm going to convince her to make me a German Chocolate Cake with Rum."

"That's a wonderful idea. I will have all the ingredients ready for you in an hour."

"Thanks, Connie. In the meantime, I will get her to take a shower and change into some fresh clothes."

"Sounds like a plan. I'll see you soon." We then hang up, and I stand to my feet.

"Time to get Dianella back on her feet." I walk out of my study and head for the second floor when I receive a phone call on my cell.

"Wilson," I answer.

"Hey, Lamonte. This is Jason. How's she doing?"

"I'm about to do an intervention. She got to get out of bed. I decided to get her to bake a cake. She says it usually helps her stay calm and collective."

"Okay, cool. Let me know if I can do anything. She got like this when Big Mama died. She doesn't take death very well. But I know my sister; she will bounce back with a swift kick in the ass. So you got to be firm with her. She will fight back but will give up after a while."

"Okay, thanks for the advice. Wish me luck. I have a feeling I'll need it."

"Good luck, man. I will call later when I have the whereabouts of the leader."

"Bet. Talk to you later." We then hang up, and I softly knock on Dianella's door.

"Dianella, are you awake?" I ask through the door.

No answer. I then knock again and let myself in.

"Dianella, I'm coming in whether you like it or not." I find her lying in bed with her back to the door. The curtains are pulled shut, not allowing any light to enter the room. Connie says she hasn't eaten anything in the past three days. And I can tell. All of her food left untouched on the foot of the bed.

I walk over to the curtains and open them up, letting in some much-needed light.

"What the fuck? Leave me alone." She barks out and then throws the blanket over her head.

I then pull the blanket off of her anticipating a fight. Jason said she would put up a fight, and he was right.

"Are you fucking kidding me," she gets out of bed and has to steady herself because she's so weak. She then approaches me and tries her best to swing on me but fails due to her lack of strength. She begins to fall forward, and I catch her before she plants her face on the floor.

"You can fight me all you want, but I won't stand by another day and watch you kill yourself. This is not healthy, and it has to stop now."

"Why not kill myself? No one gives a damn. I have assholes trying to kill me anyway; why not do it first?" she spits out.

"Are you fucking kidding me? Why would you even say some shit like that? You have your whole life ahead of you. This right here will not break you."

I then help her walk to the bathroom and place her on the bench near the sink so I can draw her a nice hot bath. She doesn't put up a fight; she just sits with hopelessness in her demeanor. I hate seeing her like this. I know she's more potent than this.

The bath is running, and I help her out of her clothes. She just sits there with no care in the world, like a zombie. I take her night shirt off and her panties. I pick her up and place her in the bath water. I promised her brother I would take care of her, and I intend on doing just that.

I get a fresh loofah and lather it up with her body wash. I then begin to scrub her back gently. As I continue to cleanse her, the tension in her shoulders and muscles in her back start to soothe away. Finally, she begins to relax and allows me to continue.

I feel myself getting hard, even though that's the last thing on my mind. But it's so hard to stay focused when I have such a beautiful woman in my home. I gather my wits and finish washing her. I then assist her out of the tub and help her dry off. I then guide her to the bench to brush her hair.

I always brushed my mother's hair, so I think I know how to get through the curls without hurting her. I run the brush through her hair, and she immediately responds to the gesture. I honestly don't know how I'm keeping myself under control. But if she continues like this, she just might get more than she bargained for.

After brushing her hair, I head for the closet to get her something to wear. I see a cute little sundress, grab it and head back into the bathroom.

"Dianella, can you lift your arms up so I can slip your dress over your head?" She does what I ask, then her towel falls, exposing her delectable breast.

Oh my God. I can't control myself any longer. I quickly get her dressed and practically drag her to the kitchen. She's going to be the death of me. But I can't take advantage. I have to respect her.

When Dianella and I arrived in the kitchen, Connie walks through the door.

"Well, good afternoon, suga. You look lovely on this beautiful day."

"Hi Connie," Dianella manage to say with no emotion in her voice.

"I thought you could help me make a German Chocolate cake with Rum. What do you say?" asks Connie.

Dianella looks at Connie with an expression I'd never seen on her before. It's almost like she remembers a past event or didn't under-stand what Connie was asking.

"Dianella, did you hear Connie? She would like you to help her bake a cake. Are you up for that?"

She shakes her head a little and refocuses on Connie. "Oh, I'm sorry. Yes, of course. I will help. I was just remembering Big Mama. She used to ask me to help all the time. Ms. Connie, you remind me so much of her," Dianella confesses.

"Suga, I remember all too well what it's like to lose a loved one, especially one so close to you. Be sure to cherish those moments. Never forget them."

This is the most I heard Dianella say all week. I'm glad I thought of this. Just what she needed. She leaves my side and walks over to the island where Connie has all the ingredients spread out.

"Looks like you got everything. You sure you need my help?" she asks Connie suspeciously.

"I'm always looking for a partner in crime. In fact, both of you can help."

"No problem, Connie. What do you want me to do?" I ask.

"Preheat the oven to three hundred fifty degrees Ferin height," Dianella instructs me. I look at Connie with a grin on my face.

She winks in acknowledgment.

We did it. We got her back.

Dianella takes over the kitchen, and we sit back and watch her go. This is her happy place, baking and creating new things.

Before we knew it, we were eating German Chocolate cake with Rum and drinking freshly brewed coffee. This is how things should be. I know it's going to take more time, but I think this is progress.

CHAPTER 11

DIANELLA

I'm sitting on the balcony, contemplating my life and everything that has happened. The autumn breeze is blowing and the trees swaying side to side. Linen curtains kick up in the drift giving a fresh scent of the day. The waterfall warps the serene atmosphere with splashes of droplets settling on my face.

This is the most peaceful place in this house. But then, I hear a gentle knock on the door.

"Come in," I announce.

Lamonte walks through the room and onto the balcony where I lay on a makeshift hammock I've created for myself.

"Good morning. How do you feel?" I really hate when people ask me that, but I know he means no harm. On the contrary, I believe he's genuinely concerned. After all, he just saw me at my worst, and he's still taking care of me.

"I'm doing better. I love what you've done with this balcony. I think this is my favorite spot, next to the kitchen, that is."

"I'm glad you're finding my home comfortable. I have something to ask you."

"Shoot," I might as well stop fighting him.

"How would you like to spend the weekend in Charleston?" I feel my mood light up, and I'm amazed that I can actually leave this prison, even for a moment.

"I can really leave?"

"Yes, I'll be with you, of course, but yes. I think you need a little break. What do you say?"

No need to contemplate anything. "Absolutely. When do we leave?"

"Whenever you're finished packing." I sprint to my feet and rush into my large walk-in closet. I'm so ready to get out of here. Do something. Do anything.

I grab a couple of outfits, something for every occasion. Then, I head to the bathroom and capture my toiletries, makeup, and hair products into my overnight Michael Kors bag. There's not a whole lot to do with my hair and I love that I can wear my hair curly or bone straight. It's nothing like having options and I prefer to be comfortable.

I'm all packed and ready to go within the hour. I'm so excited to finally be able to break free. I head downstairs and find Lamonte in the living area waiting for me.

"I'm all set," with my luggage trailing behind me.

"I could have retrieved your luggage."

"I know, but what would that do to my independent soul?" I smile at him.

"Touché. Let's go."

We put all of our luggage into his G Wagon Mercedes Titanium exterior and snow-white leather interior. I can get used to his cars alone . He has a high-class collection.

"So, where are we staying?" I ask while we get into the SUV, and he starts the engine.

"We'll stay at my family's Bed and Breakfast, The Quarters on King."

"Wow, I had no idea your family owned a BNB." There's a lot I don't know about this man.

"Yeah, my dad is huge on owning property. He says it's the biggest investment you can have in your life. People will always need land."

"He's right, you know. Big Mama used to say the same thing to Jason and me. She always wanted us to have more than she had. So when she left us everything she possessed, I knew then how valuable life is and making the most of who you are and what you have."

"I know my father is right; I just try my best not to tell him that."

"Why?" I ask while we head over the Talmadge Bridge.

"Well, my father is nothing more than a businessman. He will try to connect everything he does with finance or business. Like, having a father present is a transaction. What you put in is what you get out. All I ever wanted was to make him proud, but the day I told him I wanted to be a cop; was the day I lost my father."

"I don't think you've lost him. He just doesn't know how to express himself outside of business. Explain to him that you are also part of a business; you provide a service and do damn well at that. I mean, look at me. You could have gone on about your business, but instead, you took time off to protect me. I don't know too many people who would sacrifice their leave time to help someone else, let alone someone they barely know."

"I know more than you think. Remember, your brother is a good friend of mine. He has always talked about how proud he is of you, how strong you are, and how independent you've become. I might not have seen you before, but I definitely know a lot about you, and I like what I've heard and what I see."

"I had no idea my brother bragged about me like that. I mean, I know we have a strong relationship. We are definitely close; I just didn't know he talked to his friends about me. Does my brother know that we went on a date?" I ask because I know how my brother is.

"Yes, he knows."

"How did he take that because I didn't say a word to him."

"He was more worried that I would hurt you."

Curious, "Why would he think that?"

"Let's just say I wasn't always as nice to women."

"Oh, you're going to have to explain that one," mischief lacing my tone.

"I was more of a one-night-stand type of guy. I never wanted to get attached. Not sure why; it's just my preference."

"And now?"

"The possibilities are like the sky, unlimited. But then again, I never really thought about it, not until recently. I admit I want you. I desire you; I also understand you need your space."

"Are you willing to wait?"

"I am; however, I'm not sure I can wait that long. I have needs that women have taken care of quite often. This is new to me."

How in the world do I respond to that? He does have needs; I'm just not sure I'm ready to just push Lenny to the side.

Not yet anyway.

"I don't want to keep you from living your life. I don't expect you to wait for me to get my shit together."

"So, what are you saying? Go back to my life before you while you're under my roof?" he asks incrediously.

"Yeah, that's exactly what I am saying. I'm a big girl. I can handle it."

"So, let me get this straight. You want me to bring women to my home while you are a guest to satisfy my needs? Do you hear yourself right now?"

He's obviously upset while we're driving on these back roads. I didn't mean to upset him. I just don't want to hold him back.

"I just don't want to hold you back. I'm not sure if I will ever be ready, but us going to Charleston is a good start."

"Fine, whatever you say." He then drops the conversation. I really hope he understands that I will never hold him back. He deserves so much more than I can offer.

After a two-hour drive, we make it to the BNB, King & Society. The Quarters on King is located in the heart of Charleston's Historic District. It's said that the building was built in the 1800s and fell victim to Charleston's Great Fire in 1838. It was rebuilt and remodeled in the 1900s, giving it a modern style. And now Lamonte's family own it.

We enter the BNB, and it's filled with rustic fixtures and modern furniture. It has a loft upstairs and an open concept in the living area and kitchen. It's perfect for a simple getaway.

"You can have the master bedroom; I will take one of the other rooms," he mentions before leaving me in the living area. Yeah, he's pissed. But what can I say? I'm not ready.

I leave my luggage in my suite and decide to take a tour of the BNB which led me to a balcony overlooking the Shopping District.

"Oh my gosh. This is breathtaking." I wonder if he would be mad if I went out for a little while. No one knows I'm out of town, so it shouldn't hurt to just walk around, right?"

I go to knock on Lamonte's room door, but he doesn't respond. He's probably still pissed. Whatever. I'll leave a note on the kitchen counter. I want to walk around for a little while.

I leave a note on the counter, grab my purse and phone and leave the BNB, headed towards the shopping area. The weather is glorious, the sun out and a crisp air flowing through my lungs.

I decide to head towards the Farmer's Market. Finding new spices and foods is my passion. I make sure to stop at every booth because they are so unique to their brand. As I make it to the third booth, I feel a hand grab me so hard and yank me into a chest of solid brick. I prepare to scream but realize who it is.

"Shit."

"That right. What the fuck are you doing?" he demands. I've never seen him like this. Lamonte's livid.

"I was...uh...I just wanted to come to the Fresh Market. I tried asking you to come, but you were ignoring me."

"I was in the fucking shower. I get out to a fucking note on the kitchen counter. Do you realize how dangerous that was? Those assholes could be gang-raping you right now all because you want to fucking shop."

"I'm sorry. I didn't mean any harm." He finally releases his grip, and my arm is killing me. Jesus, he's strong. I start to rub my arm to soothe it. His nostrils flaring like a bull about to attack his prey.

"I didn't mean to grab you so hard. You just scared the fuck out of me. If anything happened to you..." he trails off. "Here, I will walk with you; just stay close to my side. Okay?" I nod my head. "No, I need to hear you say it."

"Okay, I will stay by your side." He then takes a deep breath to physically calm down, and we continue to walk through the market.

Once we hit every booth, we head back to the BNB with arms full of goodies. If I ever make it back to normalcy, I bought little trinkets for my loft and café. I also bought something to cook tonight. I think I owe Lamonte something good, and this may win me some brownie points.

Walking through the front door of the BNB, "Hey Lamonte?"

"Yes."

"What can I do to not make you mad at me anymore?"

"I'm not mad… I'm… I'm just frustrated."

"I would like to cook for you."

"The kitchen is yours. I have to make a couple of phone calls. I will be in the other room."

He begins to walk away. "I'm sorry, Lamonte. I never meant to hurt you."

He turns around, "I know. Just give me a second. I will be back."

"Okay," disappointed, I start cooking dinner. I know what he wants, but can I betray Lenny?

My mind then drifts back to what Amelia told me. *"Falling for Lamonte will not betray Lenny. He would want you to be happy."*

She's right. Lenny always wanted me to be happy. I decided to make Homemade Salmon Alfredo with broccoli.

After cooking, I find candles in one of the kitchen drawers. I decide to have a candlelit dinner with Lamonte, then I'll give him what he wants.

CHAPTER 12

LAMONTE

"*B*ro, your sister is going to be the death of me. Do you know she went to the fucking Fresh Market by herself? Then left me a fucking note like that was going to make things better. I was so fucking pissed with her. I'm pretty sure I scared the shit out of her."

"She probably deserved it. She has always been hardheaded and downplayed everything. But give her a chance; she'll come around."

I doubt it. After she told me to go fuck whoever I wanted, I know she doesn't fucking care about us. She's not even trying. "I doubt it, bro, but I will try not to kill your sister while she's under my protection."

We both laugh, "Please don't. Anyways, I have to go. Lily is making dinner."

"Talk to you soon. Out."

I walk back into the kitchen, and I smell something amazing cooking. I then see candles everywhere. What is going on?

"Dianella?"

"Dinner is served." Oh, my lord. Dianella walks out of the kitchen with a hunter-green lace teddy, high heels, and a sheer black robe. Her hair is draped around her shoulders, long and straight. Her breast nice and perky, and those hips, fuck, those hips. How the fuck am I supposed to concentrate on eating when I have this standing in front of me?

"Dianella, what—"

"Don't say anything. I've been a little crazy lately and wanted to do something for you and me. Something that both of us will enjoy. I want to eat dinner first, and then; I want you to sit and relax and enjoy the show."

Holy shit. Please lord. Don't let this girl be playing games with me. I hesitantly sit at the table, my eyes entirely concentrated on her. She then places a plate of salmon alfredo with broccoli in front of me. Pours me a glass of wine, then pours herself a glass of wine and sits across from me.

We say our blessings and begin to eat. I damn near inhaled my food and am now ready for dessert. Please let dessert be this fine woman in front of me.

"Are you ready for dessert?"

"Hell yeah." She flashes me a little smirk while clearing the dishes off the table. She's moving incredibly slow right now. Fuck, she's teasing the hell out of me.

Once she finishes, she turns on Motivation by Kelly Rowland on the surround sound. She then pulls out something from her pocket. What is that? Oh, shit. She climbs onto the table sitting right in front of me with her legs wide open. I dare not touch until she gives me permission, but fuck, she's driving me insane. She then places her vibrator on her pussy and turns it on, massaging her clit softly and slowly.

She's moaning and enjoying every moment of this torture.

"Dianella, baby. Please. I need to touch you."

"Not yet. I want you to experience everything I have to offer."

"Fuck, you're driving me crazy."

She then starts to massage her breast with her free hand, carefully pinching her nipples through the teddy. Finally, she reaches up to her strap and brings it down, exposing her breast.

Shit, I've waited too long for this.

"You may touch now," giving me permission. But, of course, she has no idea what she's in for.

I grab hold of her teddy, ripping it apart for better access. Fuck it, I'll buy her another. A tiny whimper escapes her lips.

I then take her pussy into my mouth, licking and sucking around her vibrator. She inserts it into her pussy while I suck. Fuck, this is so fucking hot. I had no idea she could perform like this.

"Make yourself come." She then picks up speed and continues fucking herself with her vibrator while I nip and tuck at her pink little clit.

"Oh…my…God. Lamonte, I'm coming."

"That's right, baby. Come in my mouth. I want to taste you." She then squirts all of her essences in my mouth. Fuck. She's a squirter. No wonder buddy didn't want to give this up.

Goddamnit, that's a fucking turn-on.

I can't take it no more. I need to feel her, and I need to fucking feel her right now.

I yank her off the table and take her to my room. I drop her on the bed and grab a condom out of my bag. I'm glad I came prepared.

I slide it on and shove my dick inside of her. She screams in pleasure, begging me to fuck her fast and hard.

"Please, harder, Lamonte. Harder Goddamnit," she begs, her head rolling backward out of pure pleasure.

I fucking give her what she wants, feeling my balls slapping her ass and watch her breast bounce up and down with every thrust. I've wanted this pussy for so long. Jesus, it's been too long since I've had someone. I'm about to fucking explode in her.

"Harder, fucking harder," she demands.

"Fuck Dianella, I'm about to come."

"No, not yet." She pulls me out and pulls me to the bed. Shit, I didn't know she was that strong. She then snatches the condom off and sucks my dick.

"Oh, my fucking God," I yell through clenched jaws.

"I want you to come in my mouth. It's my turn to taste you." And just like that, I explode from the depths of my balls into that pretty little pink mouth waiting to take all of me.

"Fuck, Dianella. I'm coming." She then sucks all of my seed out of my soul and spills it down her throat. Jesus fucking Christ. I had no idea. No fucking idea.

She licks her lips, climbs on me, and straddles my hips.

"Do you forgive me?"

"Hell yeah. How can I not? Jesus, that was the best sex I've ever had. Where the fuck did you learn all of that?"

"A woman never reveals her secrets. Just know there's more where that came from." I then wrap my arms around her waist and take her lips into mine.

"I'm glad I waited."

"I'm glad you did too."

We then drift to sleep with her lying on top of my chest.

CHAPTER 13

DIANELLA

*I*t's morning…I think. Whatever the time, my clit is being sucked, and my nipple pinched. I moan through my grogginess and run my fingers through the softest curls I've ever felt.

If this is a dream, I never want to wake up.

I open my eyes and witness the sexiest vanilla cream drop going down on me. My goodness, how did I wait so long to experience this?

I open my legs further for him, giving him all the access he wants. His tongue, nice and plump, exploring my inner walls.

"Ah, I'm so about to come."

"Um, give it to me, baby." And just like that, I'm squirting all of my essences on his tongue.

I never knew that I could squirt like that. It's never happened before. I thought I pissed myself last night right into his mouth. I was so embarrassed. But, when he drank from me, I kept my mouth shut. And here we go again, squirting like a water faucet.

"Oh, my God. You taste so good, Dianella."

"I do?" I ask with hesitation.

"Of course, you do. Why would you ask that?" He looks up into my eyes with bewilderment and pleasure written all over his face.

"I've… I've never done that before. Like…came so much."

"Really? I thought…so you're saying I'm the only one you've done this with?"

"Yes. I'm a little embarrassed," feeling my cheeks warming to a temperature I've never felt before.

"Sweetheart. Listen to me." He gets back in the bed and lays next to me. "Never be embarrassed. I thought it was sexy as hell. I actually thought I wasn't the only one, but now that I am, Lord, help me," he chuckles.

"So, you're okay with that?" I ask self-consciously.

"A natural-born squirter…Uh, fuck yeah. It's like drinking from a fountain of peach herbal tea. Your essence is so pure. So, addictive. If I didn't like it, you would've known. I do have one question, though."

"Shoot."

"What made you change your mind?"

I knew it was coming. "Well…I really couldn't come up with an excuse anymore. I guess I was more afraid of betraying Lenny, but at the end of the day, I was leaving him. I didn't want to be a part of his past. I knew deep down I needed to protect my family, my business."

"Do you regret being with me?"

"No regrets," he intertwined his fingers in mine and wrapped his strong legs around mine. At this moment, I feel protected, safe, and content.

His phone pings with a message, and he rolls over to read the content. I see his muscles tense, and his back straighten.

"What is it?" I ask with fear in my tone. "Is everything okay?"

After taking a deep breath and a moment of silence, he finally speaks. "It's your café."

∼

We arrive at The Grind. There it stood. A building no longer full of life or expression. The Grind was a victim of an ambush. Where the tall inviting windows stood is now an empty space, glass scattered every which way. I felt a never-ending terror encircling me as I stand in what used to be alive with spirited, ambitious customers.

Lamonte gave me the gory details on the way back to Savannah. "Jason has reason to believe your café was damaged by the Eastside Boyz gang. There was evidence left behind for us to find. They want us to know you are on their radar."

I pretty much blanked everything else out of my mind. I couldn't conceive the strength to listen to it anymore.

I continue to walk through the rubble. Everything I've worked hard for, destroyed. Thank goodness for insurance, but it still hurts like a punch to the gut.

I find my mother's picture on the floor and pray that nothing happened to it. It's my only copy. I pick it up and find that it escaped the terrorism of the night. Thank God. The frame may be destroyed, but the cherished memory was never broken.

"Dianella, would you like to go upstairs to your loft?" I turn and look into those grey eyes, and I start to feel comfort in his presence. He tried to warn me of the danger I was facing, but I didn't take him seriously.

I let him guide me up the stairs, allowing him to block me from any immediate danger. Not that there's any; those guys left, like the slime, they are, in the middle of the night.

We walk through the door, and it appears that my loft was left unscathed, that is, to the naked eye. But, after doing, what we thought was a thorough search, a tech came in with a black light. The words I dread of seeing stained my private place, my sanctuary, my wall over my bed in my bedroom.

The words I choose not to repeat out loud, "One Hit That Pussy, We All Hit That Pussy," Lamonte announces for all the world to hear.

My ears ringing, shouting out all other sounds, I turn myself from the words I can't say, pull out my top drawer and throw every piece of underwear, every piece of lingerie, everything in the trash.

I feel so violated. So, used. I need to get out of here.

I can't breathe.

I can't see.

I can't hear.

I ask the forbidden question I've asked so many times, before.

"Why me?"

I'm walking up the stairs in Lamonte's home, well, my home for the unforeseeable future, leaving my luggage, purse, and everything in the car. I no longer have the desire to function. I no longer feel safe from this evil world.

How can Lamonte keep me safe from the terrors of the night? He can't. No one can.

It's time to face my fear. It's time to prepare to be gang-raped and left for dead. Then, maybe I'll see my mother and Big Mama. Perhaps I will seek what I've desired for so long, freedom from terror.

I walk into my room, close the door, and head for the tub. I need a hot bath before I offer myself on a platter. I'll need to leave in the middle of the night, so Lamonte won't stop me.

He will never let me go through with this. Hell, what man would? Is this what Lenny did to other women, rape them and, when he was finished, offer her to his buddies, his boys?

How could he be so heartless, so cold? How could he ever think these people were family?

The bath is full of bubbles and hot water. I just want to soak my sorrows away.

I didn't even say a word to Lamonte on the way home. I don't feel like being bothered.

Taking my clothes off, I step into the steamy hot water and slide down until my entire body is submerged.

I don't care about my hair getting wet or the water burning my skin. I just want to hold my breath and disappear from reality for just a moment.

I then feel strong hands snatching me from my calming state. Gasping for air, "What the hell?" I yell through bits and pieces of air, brushing water and hair from my face.

"What the fuck do you mean? Are you trying to drown yourself in the bathtub?" he yells back at me.

"No damnit. This is how I relax," I confess. "I...This...This is just too much right now," I admit. "I literally have people trying to find me, strip every piece of dignity I have, and leave me defiled. How can I not have a moment to subject myself to anything but my fate? How?"

"Dianella, you have to understand. I see people at their very worst. So, when I saw you submerged under water, the first thought was, save her, now. I know this must be a lot for you to handle but know that I have your best interest in mind."

"I know you do. Since I lost my mother and Big Mama, I've learned to cope with hard things this way. The burn of the water and the suffocation of holding my breath gives me a chance to slip into a calming state of mind. Not everyone is trying to kill themselves." Or offer themselves to a potential rapist, but he doesn't need to know that tidbit.

I grab the towel and dry off. My hair, no longer straight but curling in all directions. I look like the girl from the Brave cartoon; I'm just a tad bit older. I laugh to myself, looking in the mirror.

I really wanted to be left alone, but I see that's not going to happen now. "Would you like a glass of wine? I was going to have one once I finished putting your luggage in your room."

"Fine, why not," I respond with sarcasm, more so to the situation and not Lamonte. "Just let me put something on, and I will meet you downstairs."

"Actually, meet me on the balcony in my room. I thought we could have dinner out there."

"Okay, sure."

He walks out of the room to let me change into something comfortable. It would be nice to have dinner under the stars one last time.

CHAPTER 14

LAMONTE

There's something up with Dianella. Her demeanor, her behavior. It's just not the same as when we first met. I know she's been through a lot, but she's off. I'm trying every trick in the book to ensure she's not slipping away. But honestly, I don't want to seem like a needy bitch either.

But this girl got me doing shit I've never done before, like eating dinner on my balcony. Hell, I don't even let chicks in my room. So what's really going on?

I grab a bottle of red wine from the cellar and head upstairs. Connie made steaks and potatoes with asparagus for dinner. I make it to the third floor and find Dianella standing outside my door.

"I didn't want to invade your privacy, so I stood here until your return."

"That's sweet and all, but this is your home for the time being. You can go wherever you want."

"Are you sure about that? I mean...you were very single before I crashed into your life. I meant what I said before. You can have whomever you want in your home. I don't want to stop you from doing what you want."

What the fuck? Why the fuck does she keeps trying to throw me to some random chick? Seriously, what the fuck is her problem? Calm down, Lamonte. Calm the fuck down.

"Why are you constantly pushing me to some random broad? I'm perfectly fine with the company I have now," I guide her into my room and watch her eyes light up with astonishment.

"This is your room? Like all by yourself with no one else to share it with?"

"Yeah, why?"

"Only that your room is as big as my loft and then some. It makes no sense to have this entire house to yourself with no one to share it with."

"Yeah, people tell me that all the time. My mom wants me to find the perfect girl to give her grandbabies," I admit sarcastically.

"I'm glad I don't have that type of pressure. I have enough nieces and nephews to occupy my time." So, is she saying she never wants kids?

"So, you don't want kids?" I ask, genuinely curious.

"I never thought about it, but if you must know. I don't. My mother wasn't the best role model, and Big Mama died when I was in my teens, so I really don't think I can offer a child any wisdom or guidance," she confides in me.

We eventually make our way to the balcony, where I have garden lights and candles surrounding the table. The greenery alone makes this area feel like we are in an enchanted rainforest surrounded by beautiful trees, plants, and flowers.

"You never know what you're capable of unless you try."

"I'm not willing to gamble on a kid's life on what-ifs. And besides, I'm still young. I have plenty of time to think about this. What about you?" she asks, directing the attention on me.

"Well, I've always wanted kids; I just didn't want the relationship. Most women are only after one thing, my money."

"Well, you don't have to worry about that with me. I got my own and can definitely take care of myself, even though you and my brother won't allow me."

We both laugh and take a sip of our wine.

"Here, let's eat. I'm so hungry," she announces, wanting to change the subject. I get the feeling she really doesn't like expressing herself unless I get her in the bedroom. She's a totally different person when she's fucking me.

We sit and eat in silence. Then Connie calls over the intercom that I have a visitor. Who the hell could be here this late at night?

"Thanks, Connie, I will be right down," I announce. "Are you good to sit here for a while?" I ask Dianella.

"Oh, sure. I'll be fine."

"I'll be right back."

I head down the three flights of stairs when I run flat dab into no other than LaToya Wright. Long strands of weave flows down her back and over her ass. She's in a tight mini dress, bright and in your face, with heels so high, I don't know how she's balancing herself. Her copper skin reflects in the lights and her dark eyes burn holes into my chest. Something she always did when she wasn't sure of herself. What the fuck is she doing here?

Stopping at the foot of the stairs, "What are you doing here?"

"Now, is that how you greet everyone, or is it just me?" She says with a snicker in her tone.

"Uh, no. You just caught me off guard. Some people like to call before they pop up at someone's house."

"I did. Several times, I might add. You've never returned my calls," she says with apparent attitude and disdain dripping from her demeanor. Fuck. I don't need this shit right now.

"That should tell you something," I spit out. She should've gotten the clue that she meant nothing to me. I just needed a fix for the night. I hate clingy bitches.

"What, that you're a fucking asshole. How dare you seduce me, fuck me, and then ghost me? I deserve so much more. I just wanted to tell your fuck ass in person. Fuck you and the hoe, you fucking."

"You got exactly five seconds to get the fuck out my house."

"And what you about to do?"

"Connie, please save this bitch. I'm trying real hard."

"Fuck you, Lamonte," LaToya yells.

I stock towards her with purpose in my stance and death in my stare. I stop abruptly in front of her, inches from her face. I stare into her fearful eyes and see terror screaming behind her lids.

"Get. The. Fuck. Out. Of. My. House. I didn't call you for a fucking reason. You are nothing to me. Your pussy ain't shit to me. You've fucked the entire department, and you think I would want to make you my fucking wife. You are a worthless whore who needs to treat herself better and stop expecting others to do it for you. You have exactly five seconds to get the fuck out," I whisper in her ear for no one to hear other than her and me.

I see tears running down her face, and she seems genuinely hurt by my confession, like swords slicing through her heart. She stumbles back but catches herself. She pivots on her feet and runs out the door without looking back.

Shit, I'm a fucking asshole. I turn to head to the third floor, and to my surprise, the one person I did not want to witness that encounter standing before me, Dianella.

The horror in her eyes is slicing through my very bones. I reach for her, but she stumbles back on the stairs. She turns and runs to the second floor.

"Dianella, wait," I yell after her. I take the stairs two at a time behind her, catching her at her door. "Please let me explain."

"There's no need. I told you. You can have whoever you want at your home," she declares. Then proceeds to walk into her room.

I grab her by the arm and spin her around. She comes crashing into my chest, and my dick awakens the moment I touch her. The connection we have is impossible to deny. I crush my lips to hers and fight through her resistance. I know she wants this as much as I do.

She finally opens up and softens in my arms. I explore her soul with my tongue and her body with my hands.

Every time I touch her, I feel like a horny fucking teenager all over again. I need so much more from her.

I guide her through the door and onto the bed, never losing the connection between our bodies. She let me continue my pleasurable assault as if she was never mad at me, to begin with.

She talks a big game, but deep down, she wants this as much as me.

She rips her lips from mine with a loud smack, and I immediately felt lost without her.

"No. I can't do this. I heard everything you said to that girl. How could you?"

Shit, I knew she heard something, "Here, just let me explain, and if you still don't want to speak with me, I understand." She sits quietly and lets me proceed with my explanation.

Here goes nothing. "Do you remember when I told you that most women are only after one thing when it comes to me?" She nods. "Well, LaToya is one of those women. I've been in a dark place for a long time and really only needed women for an occasional fix. She knew this before we did anything; she thought she could change me. She had to learn the hard way.

"Okay, I get that; however, that's no way to treat anyone. That statement alone could destroy a person's self-confidence, their motivation for living. You can't be one way with me and something totally different with other women."

"Trust me, I know. I'm trying to change. Believe it or not, but you are the first woman I had a desire to be different." I grab her hands and hold them in my lap, praying that she understands I will never hurt her. Pouring my soul out to her is more than I've ever bargained for, but I'm willing to do anything to win this girl's heart.

"I just need a little time to think." The final nail in my coffin. The words I never want to hear again from this woman.

And I watch the walls erected around her before my very eyes.

CHAPTER 15

DIANELLA

*W*hat Lamonte said to that girl was just terrible. I get why he did it, but my gosh, he can be very heartless. I've decided to eat my dinner on my balcony for tonight. I can't deal with him right now. And I need to get back to work soon before I have no business to return to. I have a lot of cleaning and rebuilding to do.

My phone pings with a message, which is odd since I haven't used it since Lenny died. Curious, I pick it up and read the content.

Maggie: *Hey Dianella, can you meet me at the grind? I have something to discuss with you.*

That's odd; why can't Maggie just call me. So I dial her number, and it goes straight to voicemail, so I texted her back.

Me: *Is everything okay?*

Me: *Why aren't you answering the phone?*

Maggie: *I broke my phone. I can only use the text app.*

Me: *Oh, okay. I will be there soon. I just have to let Lamonte know.*

Maggie: *No, please don't tell him.*

Maggie: *I don't want him to get involved.*

Me: *He's not going to let me leave the house. Are you able to come here?*

After a little while, she responds.

Maggie: *Okay, I will be there in a few. What's the address?*

Me: *204 Oglethorpe Ave.*

I decide to go tell Lamonte that Maggie is heading over. I hate that I have to run my every move with him. As I reach the third floor, I hear a loud crashing sound coming from the first floor.

"What was that?" I say out loud. I decided to see what fell when Lamonte grabbed me by the arm and shoves me into his bedroom.

"Stay here, call your brother. Do not open this door for any reason."

"What's wrong. What's going on?"

"Someone tripped the silent alarm." He has his gun in his hand and another in his back waistband. "Do not open this door for any reason. I will come back to get you."

"Okay, I understand." He looks at me one more time and then walks out of the room, closing the door behind him.

I start pacing the floor and remember I need to call Jason. So I dial his number, and of course, he answers on the first ring.

"Hey, Dianella."

"Jason, someone broke into Lamonte's house. He told me to stay in his room on the third floor. Then, he told me to call you."

"I'm on my way. Do as he says. Do you hear anything?"

"No, it's very quiet." And then I hear gunfire erupting in the home. "Oh my gosh! I hear gunfire. Please hurry up!"

"I'll be there soon." I then hear glass break from Lamonte's balcony.

"Jason, please hurry. There's someone coming...."

CHAPTER 16

LAMONTE

I count at least six guys running through my first floor. All wearing hoodies and face masks, trashing my home.

I don't ask questions; I just shoot, hitting three during my assault. Three down, three to go. Like the thugs they are, they return fire, aiming at nothing and missing everything.

I purposely wait for them to run out of ammo. Then, once I hear the deadly silence slicing through the air, I take back my home, leaving five dead and one wounded on my floor.

"Get the fuck up, you little bitch," coughing up blood and crying like a little pussy.

"Please…don't. I have a family."

"Fuck you and your family. You fucking come into my home and try to kill me. Why shouldn't I end you right now?"

"We just want the bitch. White Hallucination wants her alive. That's all I know," coughing up more blood.

I hear someone come through the door, and I raise my gun. "Fuck, Jason."

"Where's Dianella?"

"She's upstairs. I told her to stay in my room."

"No, man. She called me, and I was talking to her, and then the phone went dead."

"Fuck. Watch this fucker." I turn to run up the stairs, two at a time. I bust through my bedroom door and see glass scattered everywhere on the floor. I see shit knocked down, and Dianella is nowhere in sight.

I check the bathroom, walk-in closet, my gym, and my fucking office. "Fuck, they took her." I head back to my room to see if there were any clues. Fucking nothing.

I run back downstairs. "Fuck, Jason. She's gone. They fucking took her. I walked right into that trap. I'm a fucking idiot."

"We'll get her back. We must be smart about it and pray we aren't too late."

"Where the fuck did they take her?" I spit out to the little bitch on the floor.

"I don't know."

"The fuck you don't. Get the fuck up." I yank him off the floor and hold him by his worthless collar.

"Either you fucking talk or you fucking die. Which one do you prefer?"

"I promise, man. I don't know anything. White Boi never tells us his plans. He just tells us what to do, and we do it. We never know the outcome. But, he does let us have some fun though."

"What kind of fun?"

"Usually girls, weed, or drinks."

"And where does this go down?"

"In the back room of an old garage on Montgomery St. But he has cameras everywhere. You'll never get passed his security. Can I go now?"

"Yeah, you can fucking go, straight to fucking jail."

"Fuck, man."

"At least your bitch ass is still alive."

"Not for long; he's going to kill me. Especially if he knows I gave you all of this."

"That's a chance you'll have to take."

I throw his worthless ass back on the ground to bleed the fuck out.

"Jason, you got all of that?"

"Yeah, Kim is headed to the address now. You go. I will take care of this."

"Thanks, man."

"Get my sister back."

I then turn and jump into my Mercedes. "I'm coming, Dianella. Just hold on a little while longer."

CHAPTER 17

DIANELLA

"Ugh, my head and back hurt so much," I grunt softly to myself. Where am I? What happened?

I try to open my eyes and look around through my pounding head and achy body. It's so dark, but I see a little light from the door's cracks. I feel about, and I'm on a hard floor, maybe wood or tile. I can't tell.

I try to get up, but something is holding me down by my ankle. A chain maybe, I can't tell right now.

Everything starts to flood back into my memory. A man came through Lamonte's balcony of his bedroom. He had a mask on, but I could tell he was a white guy by his hands.

I fought back as hard as possible until he stuck me with something. Yes. It was a needle in my neck. I feel on my neck, remembering the pain from whatever flowed in my veins.

"Well, they found me. I knew it would be only a matter of time before they caught me. And to think, I was going to offer myself to them," shaking my damn head.

I hear voices, and then I hear the door unlock. Blinded by the light, I cover my eyes with my sore arms. Whoever it is, pushes someone else in the room with me. I back up against the wall, ready for whatever comes next.

The door slams shut, and I hear crying in the opposite corner. "Hello?" I whisper.

"Dianella, is that you?"

"Maggie?" I ask.

"Oh my gosh. What's going on? A group of guys snatched me from the café, told me to text you or they would kill me, and threw me in here. Dianella, I'm so scared," she cries out.

"Shhh. You have to be quiet. They may hear you. I think these guys are after me. Lenny, my ex, was mixed up with them, and now that he's gone, they want me. I'm so sorry I got you into all of this. I tried to protect you and Christy. That's why I haven't been to work in a couple of weeks."

"What do they want to do with us?"

"My guess, gang rape us. But to be honest, I'm not really sure," I admit.

"Oh my God. Please lord, don't let them do this to us," she prays.

"Maggie, listen to me. I'm the one they want. I will not let anything happen to you. I promise."

"You can't promise that. If they want us, they will have us," she cries out.

She's right. I can't promise they won't have their way with both of us. This is what these assholes do.

We hear voices again, and Maggie scoots closer to me like I can really protect her from the hell we're about to experience. I wrap my arms around her, and we hold each other for dear life. The door unlocks, and walks in is an older white guy, clean-shaven, grey streaks through his full head of hair. He has eyes the color of emerald shards of ice. He stands about six foot two, dressed to a T.

My breathing picks up because, for a moment, I think it's my brother, Jason, coming to save us. But, no, not this guy. This guy is the same person who has come into my café a couple of times. The guy who orders black coffee and then leaves without saying a word.

Who is he? What does he want?

"Take that one. Leave the crier here. We'll deal with her later."

"No, please don't leave me. Please, I beg you," Maggie cries.

"It's okay. Stay strong." I look into her eyes and try my best to encourage her through body language.

Someone grabs me by my arm, forcing me to stand up.

"Take the chain off her, you idiot," the white man says. "Must I tell you everything?" obviously frustrated with his men.

The young boy, not even old enough to drink, unlocks the chain around my ankle. I don't fight back because I really don't care anymore. What's the point? The only thing I want right now is to get Maggie out of this hellhole.

"Take her to my room," the white man spits out.

The time has finally come. I no longer have to be terrified of my every movement anymore. The young boy guides me down a hall of concrete. There are closed doors on both sides, secured with padlocks on them. The smell is God awful, with a strong odor of urine, mildew, and dead animals. It's so cold and damp. We enter a room that is the total opposite of what I just witnessed. The walls are entirely purple with black leather furniture, with a black king-size bed in the middle. Candles are flickering everywhere, and the smell of fresh orchids teases my senses. The boy places me on a black leather sofa and leaves the room to make me wait for my demise.

CHAPTER 18

LAMONTE

$\mathcal{M}$y phone rings, and I pick it up without even looking at the caller ID. "Yeah."

"It's Knight. I have some information you and Jason may want to hear."

"He's not with me. He's still at my house. What's up?"

"Hold on, I will patch him through. You both need to hear this."

Shit, something is up. Why else would she want to include Jason?

"Hey, are y'all both there?"

"Yes," I say.

"Yeah, go ahead," Jason says.

"Okay, now that I have you both on this call. I found out something that is a little weird. I cross-referenced White Hallucination, the property's address, and the owner. Apparently, a Johnathan and Samantha Hall own the property. Samantha died several years ago, leaving two young children alone after her husband, Johnathan, left them. The children are—"

"Jason and Dianella Hall. What are the fucking odds?" Jason blurts out. "Are you sure about this, Kim?"

"Yes, I'm sure."

"Hold on, what are y'all saying?" I ask, confused.

"The garage you're about to raid is owned by Dianella and Jason's father," Kim says.

"What the fuck?" I pipe up.

"My thoughts exactly," Kim says. "Jason, I know you don't really know your father, but can you give us anything to go on? I'm still pulling information that may help."

"I haven't seen my father in over twenty years. I never bothered trying to find him. I didn't want to. After he left us, I erased him from my memory altogether. I never thought about the fact that he may still be in town. It never occurred to me."

"Well, we need you to think hard and fast. Dianella needs us, and we don't know if your father is involved or not," I say.

"Don't you think I know that? I've been dealing with this shit a lot longer than you have. So, back the fuck off," Jason spits out.

Fuck, he's right. He is going through all of this just as well as I am. Learning about your father still being in the area after all of this time has to be devastating.

"Sorry, man. I didn't mean to be a little bitch. I'm just concerned about Dianella and need to get her back."

"No sweat. I just never considered that my father could be involved. Kim, do we have anything else about my father?"

"Well, it looks like he never really left the Savannah area. He has done some traveling, though. It looks like he travels back and forth from here to South Carolina quite often. He has property here and in South Carolina, like strip clubs, bars downtown, and the garage in

Midtown Savannah. However, his permanent home appears in Hilton Head, South Carolina. I will do some more digging.

"Lamonte, in the meantime, check out that garage. There's a neighborhood across the way. It's Sylvan Terrace neighborhood. I will be on my way once patrol takes this guy," Jason says.

"Sure thing."

CHAPTER 19

DIANELLA

*S*oft music plays while mist of lavender and lilac drifts through the air. I look around the room and find silver chains hanging from the bedpost with leather handcuffs on each chain. On the opposite wall, I see a chest of different types of sticks and whips.

I crawl into a ball on the couch because I have no idea what I've gotten myself into. Is he going to torture me? What kind of room is this? Was Lenny really into this type of shit?

I hear the door open, and my heart slams through my chest, causing severe pain in my every labored breath. I no longer want to die; not like this.

"Hi, sweetheart."

"Hi," my voice sounding so small under my pounding heart.

"Would you like something to drink? Say a glass of wine or a shot of whiskey?" What the hell? Do I really look like I want a drink? I stare at him blankly. "I'm not asking."

He pours me a glass of red wine and hands it to me. He then pours himself a glass and sits next to me with this wicked grin on his face.

"Who are you?" I ask.

"Who do you want me to be?"

"I've seen you before. You've come to my café a couple of times. What do you want?"

"I want you. I've always wanted you."

Fuck. This is more twisted than I thought. All this time, I felt entangled with fear of the assholes who killed Lenny, but I should have been afraid of this guy.

"Why do you want me? I don't know you, and I have nothing to offer you. Just, please let me and my friend go, and I promise I won't say anything."

"You really don't have a clue as to why you're here."

"Should I?"

"You should."

"Look, I'm not a game-playing type of girl. Just tell me what you want and get it over with. I seriously don't give a shit anymore," I confess even though I'm scared shitless out of my mind.

"Feisty, I like. Just like your mother."

"What? What does my mother have to do with this?" I ask, thoroughly confused.

"I'm glad you asked. Now we're getting somewhere. Your mother was a breath of fresh air, beautiful, smart, and feisty to the bone. She didn't take any shit from anyone. Samantha was a bitch from hell, but I couldn't get enough of her. Until, well, you know the rest."

"Actually, I don't know the rest. My mother died when I was young. So I knew nothing about her."

"So, you're telling me that bitch didn't even enlighten you with your history?"

"What bitch are you referring to?" I ask.

"Dianella, my dear. You are really in the dark. How interesting."

"In the dark about what?"

"I'm your father, dear."

CHAPTER 20

LAMONTE

*J*ason really needs to hurry the fuck up. The longer we sit dicking around, the longer Dianella has to endure torture from those assholes.

Sitting across the street at an abandoned house, I have a direct view of the garage. I see at least four lookouts walking the perimeter of the grounds, two standing at the front entrance and two standing at the back, with a total of six men on surveillance. I have no idea how many are inside the garage.

My phone starts to vibrate. It's Kim. "Hey, what you got for me?"

"The Eastside Boyz have about sixty men and twenty women in their gang. There are two chapters with White Hallucination as their leader. Each chapter has a president and a vice president. The women are merely there for sexual favors. If a brother starts a relationship with a woman, he must invite her to the brotherhood. In order for her to be vetted, she must offer herself to all brothers of the chapter. Most women don't and are ultimately cast out. But those who survive the brutal test become offerings to their leader who will vet them to become sisters of the brotherhood."

"Wow, that's really fucked up."

"Yeah, it is. My guess is that Lenny did not want Dianella to be a part of that culture, so he kept their relationship a secret. When he stopped going to the mandatory fellowships, the vice president started looking into his absences, and I'm thinking they found out about Dianella, which led to his death. Not vetting your girlfriend through the brotherhood is a deathable offense. He paid the ultimate price to protect her."

Shit, I did not want to hear that right now. Why he couldn't be a fuck boy or some shit. He actually fucking cared about her.

"So, why fuck with her now? He already paid the price."

"They are not known to keep their word. Because he had her, they want to have a piece of her."

"Well, fuck that. They have to get through me before that fucking happens."

Jason pulls up as Kim, and I hang up.

"Hey, bro. We got at least six outside. I'm not sure about the inside. But I ain't waitin' on no backup. We got to get her out of there now."

"I agree, but we can't be stupid either. We don't know what we're up against. That's why I called the Strategic Investigation Unit. They've been investigating this crew for months now. They have a hell of a lot more information than we do. Six dudes then walk up from the cut. Lamonte, this is Sgt. Jordan and his team, Patricks, Howard, Johnson, Sims, and Young. They will be helping us get Dianella back. Sarge, the floor is yours," Jason says.

"Thanks, Hall. These guys are smart. They are always three steps ahead of us in every operation. We haven't been able to breach their walls, but now they've messed up. I don't know what it is about your sister, but this is out of the norm for them," Sgt. Jordan says.

"What information do you have on the leader?" I ask, ignoring that little comment.

"White Hallucination, aka WH, aka White Boi. He's old school. Does everything through beepers and landlines. He only believes in technology when it comes to his surveillance. His real name is Johnathan Hall...."

"Hold the fuck up. My father is the leader of this fucking gang? What the fuck?"

"You didn't know that?" Sgt. Jordan asks.

"Fuck no. We just thought he owned the property. What the fuck is going on?" I ask.

"Oh, shit. You are in for a real fucking treat then. He's a real piece of work. He has his boys do all the dirty work, keeping his hands clean, prostitution, drugs, and money laundering. You name it, he has his hands in it. His new adventure is an underground sex trafficking ring. We almost had one of our men make it in, but he got injured, and we had to pull back. This is as close as we've ever been to getting inside that garage. We will definitely need firepower. They are heavily armed and young and stupid. Which means they don't give a shit about anything or anyone. Are y'all game for this?"

"Fuck yeah. We need to get Dianella back sooner than later," I demand.

"Then, let's go. Remember, this is off the books. Cap will have a shit storm once he finds out we are operating off the books."

"Yeah, we know. We will deal with him later. But, right now, my sister is all that matters," Jason says.

"Then let's do this," I say.

I honestly do not know how I got myself into this shit, but there is definitely something different about this girl. I'm to the point of lying my life on the line with no questions asked. Did not ever see this coming.

We begin loading our guns and strapping with Kevlar. Time to prepare for war or whatever the hell we about to walk into. Who the hell knew that Dianella and Jason's father was behind all of this shit? I hope the God he's not because this is not going to end well.

CHAPTER 21

DIANELLA

"*Here, sweetie, come have a seat on Big Mama's lap.*"

Big Mama is so nice. Jason, of course, is a stupid head to her. But she still is the nicest lady in the world. She gives me candy and toys, and she also reads to me at night. Mommy did good this time. She picked a cool lady to watch us.

I climb on Big Mama's lap and twirl my hair between my fingers. Jason is sitting on the floor playing with his GI Joes.

"Look it here, my little ones. Yo, mama ain't comin' back. She wit God now, and there's nothin' you can do 'bout it. Now let's pray together." Big Mama says.

"Where is she?" I ask.

"She in heaven now," Jason says.

"But why? She don't want us anymore?" I ask.

"No, and that fuck tard don't want us neither," Jason snaps.

"Watch yo mouth, boy," Big Mama says sternly through clenched teeth. "We ain't 'bout to cuss 'round here. Understand, boy?"

"Yes, ma'am," Jason says, then bows his head in defeat. "He just left us, and now look. We don't have nobody. What are we supposed to do?"

"You look after each other. I'm always here to guide you, but you two are blood. You remember that. Here, Dianella, get down and play with your dolls. Let me talk wit yo, brother."

I climb down and playhouse with my barbie dolls.

"Jason. I know yo daddy left y'all. And that's a shame, but you can't keep that bottled up. You gotta let it out. You hear. Anger will eat you alive."

"But I seen him. He was with that redhead woman. He was having sex with her, and mama was lying on the floor the whole time. He did something to her. I know it. I know he killed her. We have to tell the police the truth. We have to, Big Mama," Jason cries out.

"Jason, baby, the cops already know. He got them wrapped 'round his finger. He can't get in trouble 'bout nothin'. I here to protect you and yo sister. That man won't be bothering y'all no mo."

Jason climbs into Big Mama's lap, and she rocks him to sleep. Just like I do with my baby dolls. She really loves us. Mommy did a great job.

Holy shit, did he kill our mother? Is this what he's talking about? What the fuck is going on?

"Ah, I see the light bulb flashing in those beautiful eyes. You remember, don't you?"

"Did you kill our mother?"

"I wouldn't say kill. That's a strong word. I helped her along the path she wanted to be on."

"What the fuck does that mean?"

"Your mother disagreed with the life I wanted to have for us. She felt it was, what was the word she used, ah, yes, sinful. Your mother left her home at a young age. Her parents were very abusive toward her, and she couldn't take it anymore, so she left. I met her soon after that. When I tell you, your mother was the most beautiful creature

I've ever seen. She was absolutely stunning, with beautiful green eyes. She had long wavy brown hair, the fantasy of every man's wet dream. When she took my order at the Bayou Café, I fell dick first in lust. She was a fine piece of ass."

What a fucking prick. I can't believe I have to stand here and listen to this shit.

"Anyways, back to the good stuff. Your mother could not handle life in general, so I gave her a little boost. She was doing very well until she caught me fucking other women. Shit went downhill from there. All she had to do was let me do what I needed, and everything could have been just gravy."

"So, what are you saying? I can't keep up with your reasoning for whatever the fuck this is."

"I run a business, my darling, and everything that comes through my business must be tested."

"What's that supposed to mean?"

"Your life no longer belongs to you. It belongs to me, and until I test my product, you will remain here until you are sold. I have bidders lined up waiting to taste that sweet pussy of yours. You see, your mother was my property. I brought her from that little café on River Street. Her main fucking goal was to produce girls for me to sell, and she fucked that up by overdosing. Little bitch. And then sent y'all somewhere where I couldn't find y'all. Oh, she got me good. But things happen to come to circle. What a fucking coincidence that you would be fucking one of my guys and come prancing back into my life anyway. What are the fucking odds.?" Johnathan brags with a gut-wrenching chuckle that creeps within my bones.

Oh my God, I'm about to be sick. What the fuck have I done?

I double down and throw up everything I ever ate. Vomit splashing everywhere.

"You can vomit all you want. You're cleaning that shit up. You have one hour, and then we're leaving."

"Wait, what about Maggie? Please let her go. She has nothing to do with this," I beg.

"I will let her go if you bend over right now and let me fuck you."

Shit, fuck. I can't do that. But I can't let her receive the same fate as me. I just can't.

He turns to walk out— "Wait, I'll do it. I will give you what you want. Just, please let her go."

"Bend over."

"Promise me, Goddamnit."

"Fine, I fucking cross my heart. Now, bend the fuck over."

"Lamonte, I'm so sorry. This is all my fault," I whisper to myself.

I pull my pants down and bend over on the bed like he asked.

I can't believe my father is about to rape me, and there is nothing I can do about it. I did ask for this, but not like this. Not my father raping me and taking everything from me. I was fucking okay with little boys hittin' it, but not this.

Not my own father...

I feel him come behind me, and he touches my ass as if he's admiring his work, his creation. He then walks away, and I hear a lock or something. I dare not look. I have no idea what he has in store for me.

He then approaches me from behind again, and this time I feel something wet squirted into my asshole. "Oh, God, please don't. Not my ass. Please," the realization hitting me like a dump truck slamming into a solid brick wall.

"Ah, yes, I love it when a bitch beg."

Shit, please, God, take this pain away. Please let me feel anything else but this. Please, God.

He slams through my tightness, ripping me apart. Screaming at the top of my lungs, I slip into a state of darkness. Forcing myself to focus on anything but the torture I'm about to endure.

Everything around me starts slithering away. The lights, the colors, the sounds, and the smells gone like flipping a cartoon book of emptiness.

I feel so alone, so lost, so abandoned. How can God let this happen to me? How can anyone do this to their own daughter? I'm nothing to him. He hates me that much; he's willing to rape me, sell me, and then just what, get rid of me.

It feels like hours have passed, and he's still pumping his massive dick inside of my ass, depleting anything that I ever had or wanted in life. My body slamming through the bed, my head banging on something so hard, I'm not even sure of anymore, whelps piercing my skin with every slash on my back. I no longer feel pain but numbness drifting through my veins. My eyelids become heavy, and my heart rate has slowed to a simple flutter.

I'm awaken to someone else deflowering my body, bruising my milky skin, and I don't care anymore. My eyes flutter shut again as another has his way with me, and another and another...

Soon, I forget how many has taken from me.

I don't want to know anymore.

Am I dying?

If only it could be that simple. If only I could at this very moment. Now, I know precisely what Lily and Kim went through. Now, I understand why they will never open up to this horrific nightmare. Now, I know the true meaning of losing everything, your soul, mind, and body.

Now, I'm entangled with nothing.

Not to Lenny.

Not to Lamonte.

Nothing.

CHAPTER 22

LAMONTE

*T*here are eight of us, and we might not survive, but as long as I save Dianella from this hell hole, I don't give a fuck.

We slither through the night, taking one to two men out at a time. Eight down, God only knows how many are left to kill. Sarge and his crew enter first, Jason and I on their heels. Gunfire erupts through the night, leaving bodies in their tortured path. Finally, we make it to the basement with a long hallway of steel doors. Shooting every last lock off in our way.

We enter one of the doors and find a young girl curled up in the corner. She has only a long tee-shirt on, no shoes, no pants. She's filthy, with dirt and grime all over her body. She's so skinny; I can literally see her bones. The smell alone makes me want to vomit everything I've eaten.

She has to be no older than thirteen.

"My God, what have they done to this poor girl?"

"My guess raped her, beat her, and drugged her repeatedly," Jason answers.

"How does this type of shit turn anyone on is beyond me? You got to be a sorry motherfucker to do some shit like this?" I spit out.

"Yeah, I know. We have several more rooms to go. I gotta bad feeling there will be more just like her," Sarge announces.

Fuck, Dianella. Hold on, baby. We're coming. Just hold on a little while longer.

We clear at least twenty more rooms with twenty more girls in each, either dead or half dead. We then come to one last room, and I'm almost afraid of what we'll find. Jason shoots off the lock; I enter the room, and then a woman jumps into my arms.

"Oh my God, thank you, thank you, thank you so much for saving me."

"Maggie, is that you?" Jason asks.

"Oh, Jason, thank God you are here. They took Dianella somewhere and left me here. I have no idea what they are doing to her. You got to find her. This is all my fault," Maggie cries out while clenched to my neck.

"Why is this your fault?" I ask Maggie.

"They made me text her so they could find out where she was. They said if I didn't text, then they would kill me. I believed them. They then took my phone and brought me here."

"Did you notice anything else about the people who took you?"

"They were really young, like teenagers. They all were drinking and getting high. Once I got here, an older white guy came in here. He took Dianella with him and said he would deal with me later. I'm not sure where they went."

"Here, go with this officer. He will get your statement and then take you home. If you can remember anything else, call me at this number," I hand her my card, and she leaves with Officer Young.

"Fuck, they couldn't have gone far. Where the fuck are they?" I ask more of myself than the others.

"I don't know, man, but we will find her. I fucking wish she didn't fight me on that tracking device. That was the only way I could find Kim, Lily, and Amelia. Dianella refused to wear it, saying it was intrusive to her life. Now, look at her. Fuck," Jason spits out.

"Look, man, we gotta keep it together. She needs us right now. What else do we know about this guy?" I ask.

"Hey, there's another door over here. It looks like it leads to another room or hallway," Officer Patricks announce.

Jason and I take off towards the area. Jason shoots off the lock, and I kick the door in.

"Jesus Christ!"

CHAPTER 23

DIANELLA

*I*t's the perfect day, sun shining bright, wind blowing through my strands, flowers delivering a delectable smell. I'm relaxing in Forsyth Park with a good book and the perfect glass of wine. Lamonte spending the day with me while our children run and play on the swing set. I'm completely connected to all that is, accompanied by family and the man who makes everything okay. Just to be next to him, holding his hand, gives me life in my soul.

"Get up," I hear in the distance, snatching me away from my perfect day. "Get the fuck up. Don't let me have to say it again," I hear again.

No, I don't want to leave. Please don't take me from my perfect day.

I feel ice-cold water drench my face and clothes. I jump up immediately and feel a sharp pain in my back. "Ouch, shit, that hurts," I cry out.

"Maybe next time you will do as I say. I need you to get dressed and meet me downstairs. You have one hour," Johnathan demands and then walks out, shutting the door behind him.

I look around because I have no idea where I am... once again. The room is actually gorgeous with a wooden plank accent wall and light green walls. All the furniture is white, including the bed and bedding. I see there's a bathroom in the corner with a large garden tub. There's a large walk-in shower in the corner and a large walk-in closet filled with women clothes.

I begin to take my clothes off, slowly, utterly shocked at the amount of blood drenched through each shred. "What did he do to me?"

That can't possibly be all mine.

I turn the hot water on in the shower and stand underneath for what seems forever. The heat opens my pores completely, letting the water wash off all the sins that occurred to me overnight. Honestly, I can't even remember what happened to me; I just feel the horrific pain.

I continue to wash my hair and body. I then step out to the most dreadful sight in my life. The reflection in the mirror looks nothing like me. This body, those bruises can't belong to me. What did he do to me? I turn a little to see my backside even though I know I will be horrified by what I see.

Bruising in a way that I thought wasn't possible. My back is completely covered with handprints and whelps. I have swelling everywhere, my skin broken, blood seeping through the slits. How the fuck am I even standing? I have to get out of here.

And now.

I snatch a pair of jeans out of the closet and a clean tee shirt. I find a pair of socks, underwear, and a sports bra in the drawer. I slide on some shoes, throw my hair into a ponytail, even though it's extremely painful to do so; and run straight for the window. There's no fucking way I'm staying here and letting this crazy fucker kill me.

To my surprise, the window opens easily. I'm at least two stories high. If I jump, I may break an ankle or something, but at least I have a chance to get away. I throw my legs over the ledge and pray that I don't break anything on the way down. I slide out the window, falling into some bushes right under the window. I bend my legs on impact, preventing any long-term effects. I get up and dust myself off, feeling a sharp pain in my side. I hear voices headed towards me, so I duck back in the bushes.

I have at least twenty more minutes before they realize I'm gone. The two men, or boys from the looks of it, pass by joking around, carrying guns across their bodies. What has the world come to? They can't be no more than fifteen years old.

Once they pass by, I hightail it to the property's gate. I have no idea where I'm going, but it got to be better than this place. I climb the fence, hop over the barbwire, and land on my feet.

I then run for dear life through the darkness. Finally, after about fifteen minutes, I make it to a road, but I stay in the wood line, so those assholes won't find me. I never thought in a million years I would find myself running for my life. Thank God for all the training I do every day.

"Shit, Maggie. I can't believe I forgot about Maggie."

Think Dianella, think. I can't just leave her there. I have to help her. But, fuck, I'm free from those assholes. I can find help to get her out of that hellhole.

"Maggie, hold on. I'll come back for you. I promise."

CHAPTER 24

LAMONTE

*O*h, my God, all the blood. It's everywhere. What the fuck happened in here? Where is she? I have to find her.

I drop to my knees because I have no more fight left in me. I put my hands together and pray to God. Like really pray like my mother taught me as a young boy.

"O LORD, hear my prayer, listen to my cry for mercy; in your faithfulness and righteousness come to my relief."

"Do not bring your servant into judgment, for no one living is righteous before you."

"The enemy pursues me, he crushes me to the ground; he makes me dwell in darkness like those long dead."

"So, my spirit grows faint within me; my heart within me is dismayed."

"I remember the days of long ago; I meditate on all your works and consider what your hands have done."

"I spread out my hands to you; my soul thirsts for you like a parched land. Selah."

"Answer me quickly, O LORD; my spirit fails. Do not hide your face from me or I will be like those who go down to the pit."

"Let the morning bring me word of your unfailing love, for I have put my trust in you. Show me the way I should go, for to you I lift up my soul."

"Rescue me from my enemies, O LORD, for I hide myself in you."

"Teach me to do your will, for you are my God; may your good Spirit lead me on level ground."

"For your name's sake, O LORD, preserve my life; in your righteousness, bring me out of trouble."

"In your unfailing love, silence my enemies; destroy all my foes, for I am your servant," I cry out."

I don't care who hears me or who sees me. I've learned a good prayer for guidance and salvation will go a long way to redemption.

I stand up, and Jason embraces me with his strong arms. Any other day, this would be gay as shit, but today, he's my brother, and I need all the support I can get right now.

"Call Kim. She must have some information for us," I say.

Jason dials Kim's number and puts her on speaker for both of us to listen.

"Hey Kim, we raided the garage, finding over twenty-one women and children who are malnourished, dirty, and weak.

This is definitely a sex trafficking ring. Set up the safe shelter and DFACS to find a place for these women and children. Check the database to see if we have any missing person reports on these girls. Also, reach out to Homeland Security. They can assist with some that are from out of town."

"Okay, I'll jump right on it. Oh, by the way, Johnathan's property in South Carolina is very secluded. I would think that would be a great place to take someone without being caught," Kim says.

"Thanks, Kim. I appreciate it. Send me the location on my phone. We will check it out. In the meantime, have SIU search the other bars in Savannah. We are bound to find something in those as well," Jason says.

"Okay, and Jason, Lamonte, be careful."

"All the time."

We then hang up, brief Sgt. Jordan on our next steps, and head to the next location. I hope to God we find Dianella.

CHAPTER 25

DIANELLA

I finally recognize where I am; after wondering around for hours. The Talmadge Bridge is just a few miles ahead. Thank God. The only bad thing about this is, no wood line to protect my whereabouts. So I have to make it over that bridge without anyone finding me.

I begin to jog my way up the bridge when I see headlights coming my way. Of course, it could be anyone, but that's wishful thinking. Keep running, Dianella, keep running.

The car stops just ahead of me, and of course, Johnathan's boys jump out of the vehicle. Fight or Flight is all I think about. Stand here and let them kill you or fight the fuck back.

Fight it is.

I run full speed ahead, tackling the first boy to the ground. He slams his head to the ground, knocking him out completely. The second boy starts shooting at me, grazing my arm, but I don't feel a thing. My adrenaline is in overdrive. I snatch the gun out of his hand, shooting him in the head.

The third person steps out of the car, and it's no other than Johnathan himself.

"I underestimated you, I see."

"Fuck you."

"You've already done that."

All the hate, fear, and sorrow come pouring out of me all at once. The loss of Lenny, the loss of my sanity, the loss of my soul...all gone.

He approaches me, daring me to shoot him. Just like the cocky motherfucker he is, come strolling up to me with that smooth glide like I won't shoot his ass in the dick. I pull the trigger, and it clicks.

"Fuck." The fucking gun is empty. Time to fucking put my defensive tactics to use. Fight or die Dianella.

I stand there as calmly as I possibly can. I can't show him fear. He's taller and bigger, but you're smarter and faster. You can do this, Dianella.

"I love it when they fight back. You know what happened the last time. It will be much worse," he confesses. "I want to watch you bleed. I'm getting hard just thinking about it."

He reaches for my neck, and I sidestep, ensuring not to get hit by a car or go over the bridge. I then punch him in the throat, causing him to double over. I then punch him several times in the head, forcing him to the ground.

I get ready to stomp him when he catches my foot, twists my ankle, causing me to fall forward, slamming my face on the ground. I roll over in pain, blood splattering from my mouth and nose, everywhere. He climbs on top of me, punching me repeatedly in my stomach and face. Finally, I'm able to knock him off of me with my hips. But it takes every ounce of energy I have. I snatch the gun from his waistband and pull the trigger, shooting him three times in the chest. He falls on top of me, making it painfully hard to breathe. After a moment, I manage to push him off me with the last bit of strength I have left.

I roll over on the ground in severe pain, not realizing that I've been stabbed and barely able to keep my eyes open. Then, I hear someone call my name…

"Dianella!"

CHAPTER 26

LAMONTE

Watching Dianella there, her lifeless body on the ground, took every breath I had. It felt like someone sucker punched the shit out of me and left me to drown in my own sorrow.

I knelt down next to her, cradling her head in my arms. There's blood everywhere. I'm not sure if it's hers or theirs. I feel for a pulse, unwilling to accept that she's gone. I feel something, but my own heart is racing; I fall back on my heels, letting Jason check for me.

"Please tell me we aren't too late. Please, Jason," I beg.

"Hold on. Give me a second." I wait impatiently for him to tell me she's gone forever. "Wait, I feel something. She has a pulse, but it's fucking weak as shit. We got to get her to the hospital now."

I pick her lifeless body off the ground and carry her to the SUV, leaving that fucking prick behind. What the fuck did he do to her?

"Hold on, Dianella, baby, please hold on." Jason drives while I hold her in the back seat. She's barely breathing, and I pray we make it in time. Lord, please let us make it.

We made it to the hospital in record time, considering we were practically in another state. Jason pulls up to the bay, and there's staff already waiting on us. Jason must have called ahead of time. Hell, I've been so focused on Dianella I don't even know how we got here; which street we took, street lights, nothing. Everything is a blur, except for Dianella.

My Dianella.

Jason opens the door for me, and I place Dianella on the stretcher, watching the hospital staff take her away.

CHAPTER 27

DIANELLA

eep.

Beep.

Beep is all I hear in the background.

Beep.

Beep.

Beep.

Finding my voice, I open my eyes and see nothing but white and blue walls. I see cords and machines everywhere. The light is so bright; it's blinding me. Where am I?

"Doc, she's awake. Give her more anesthesia. She can't be waking up already," a female yelled.

"Shit, we still have hours to go. She can't possibly wake up already," another female says.

I then drift onto a serene island with untouchable beauty. Translucent turquoise seas surrounding me. I feel the sparkling white beach of sand through my toes. I smell the exotic aroma of wild flowers and fresh green alfalfa. The sound alone gives me a touch of melodious sound through my ears. I never want to leave this beautiful place. I want to stay forever.

I feel a jolt awaking my soul and ripping me from my island.

"No, please. Let me stay. I don't want to leave."

Please. Let me stay.

CHAPTER 28

LAMONTE

*I*t's been three weeks, and Dianella still hasn't awakened from her medically induced coma. I haven't left her side, and I don't plan on leaving any time soon.

Her family has come and gone daily, giving me strength through prayer. But, I will never forget what Dr. Evans told me the day we arrived.

"Dianella has suffered severe trauma to her brain and major organs. Her head was slammed so many times that it caused her brain to bleed and shift. Her left lung was pierced with one of her broken ribs, which we were able to repair; however, she may suffer some long-term effects from the attack. Both of her hands were fractured but should heal properly. She had severe trauma through sodomy, and we thought we would have to add a colostomy bag, but we think we were able to repair the tears to the lower intestine. My biggest concern is the brain injury. We will know more when she wakes up," Dr. Evans says.

My God is all I can fathom at this moment. How can anyone do this to another human being? How?

"Do know, she put up one hell of a fight. She was determined to survive. She keeps fighting like that, and she will do just fine," Dr. Evans adds as she walks out.

Left with the constant beeping sounds and the machines blaring at me, I find myself fucking crying once again, in agony.

"What the fuck is wrong with me?"

"There's nothing wrong with you, man. Trust me, I know," Jason walks in, providing an answer to my question. "I've been in this same position, in that same chair for Lily, and I can tell you, it's not easy. But you will get through it. Dianella will not reach out to you or me, but we have to stay strong for her. What happened to her is unforgivable, to say the least, but she will blame herself and fall into a deep hole."

"I can't let that happen."

"I know. That's why I'm here to support you. Tell me something. Are you in love with my sister? Like, really in love and not that bullshit about I like her a lot, blah blah blah."

"I honestly don't know. But I do know I can't live without her. I can't sleep without knowing she's okay first. I feel like a knife is stuck in my fuck chest, and I can't fucking breathe. I do know that. I've never been in fucking love. I've tried to stay away from it at all costs, but there is something about Dianella. I just don't know how to explain it. Fuck."

"Actually, man, you got it fucking bad and don't even know it. But when you do figure it out, it will change your life forever," he explains. But what I don't give two fucks about is anything else. All I care about is Dianella getting the fuck out of this hospital and tracking down the son of a bitch who put her in here.

This is my fucking fault. I let those motherfuckers come into my home and take her from me. And now look at her, fighting for her life for no reason at all. It should be me laying in that fucking bed.

It should be me.

"You hear me, man?" Jason asks, pulling me from my own personal torture.

"What?" I spit out because I really don't know or give a shit what he just said.

"Stop blaming yourself. This is not your fault either."

"How can you say those fucking words to me right now? Look at her. Just fucking look at her. That should be me." I spit out with pure venom in my tone, body language, and every being.

"It should not be you—," Kim walks in, interrupting our conversation.

"I have something, and I think you need to hear this shit." We both nod in anticipation and give her the floor.

"We got a search warrant for Johnathan's house in South Carolina. HSI helped us out on that part since it's in a different state," we both look at her like, get to the fucking point. "Anyways, Johnathan had a lockbox in his closet behind a bunch of shit. He had all his important documents in there and something you might want to read, Jason." She looks into his eyes, giving him strength; we didn't think he needed. The shit must be gnarly, or she would have waited. One thing about it, this family doesn't mind telling it like it is. I see where Dianella gets it; no sugarcoating required.

She hands over the envelope, which I can only think contains a letter or something. He reaches for it and pulls the documents out.

There are photos and what appears to be a letter. He glances at the images, and a strange dim skims over his brow. He brings the photo closure for a better view as if he doesn't already have twenty-twenty vision.

"What the—" is all he can muster up. He drops the photos, and I bend down to pick them up. There's a photo of a woman. A gorgeous woman. She has long curly auburn hair, green eyes, and a figure to die for.

I glance at the second photo, and it's a younger Lenny and this woman obviously having sex. Then another picture of Lenny, another guy, and the woman having anal and vaginal sex. But in this photo, she looks a little off, like scared and drugged. And then, the last picture shows the woman on the bed, passed out with bruising all over her body.

"What are these?" I ask, totally confused. Kim glances at Jason, but he doesn't say a word. So, she explains what I'm looking at.

"These photos are of his mother, Samantha. That's Lenny," she points to the third photo, "And that's Lenny's best friend, Jay aka Jacob," she explains. "It appears that Samantha wrote a letter to her children explaining what happened to their father and why he was never coming back. It also explains why she had to give them to Big Mama. You see, Johnathan was a sick bastard. He developed this mindset that he was a king or a God of some sort. He craved money and power, and what other way to make quick money and have power other than selling drugs and women. He wanted to experience it with his wife, Samantha, but she wasn't down. So, he made her a deal...."

"What deal?" I question, wanting her to continue.

"When Dianella was old enough, she would have to trade tricks for shelter. He wanted Jason to be his right-hand man and someday run the organization. That's when Samantha sobered up enough from the drugs he was feeding her and went to Big Mama to take Jason and Dianella and raise them. You see, Big Mama was Samantha's guardian as well. Johnathan never knew because she never spoke about her past. All he knew was she was in foster care because her parents abused her, and she didn't want her children to have the same fate. Big Mama was her saving grace; she knew she would be theirs."

"Holy fucking shit," is all I can muster at this moment.

The room is silent except for the beeping from the machines. I stare at Dianella in a whole new light. I can only imagine what the fuck she went through.

Jason finally speaks, "What in the fucking hell? Big Mama never mentioned any of this shit." He gets up and walks out.

"Kim—"

"I got him. Stay here with Dianella. She will need you when she wakes up." I nod in agreement, not really caring about anything else but her right now.

Can I actually be in love with her?

Am I capable of being selfless and loving another person?

How the fuck did I get here?

Questions flooded my mind with no answers in return. Jesus, help me. I have no more strength to think.

CHAPTER 29

LAMONTE

*a*nother fucking three weeks, and Dianella still hasn't woken the fuck up. People coming and going, paying their respects while I sit here getting angrier by the fucking second.

The fucking doctors keep trying to reassure Jason and me that she will wake up from this hell. But, unfortunately, she just doesn't want to right now.

I think that's a load of bullshit. Why wouldn't she want to come back? Back to me? I can't fucking accept that. Not now, not ever.

"Dianella, baby, please come back to me. I can't fucking eat. I can't fucking sleep. Shit, I'm losing my fucking mind right now. I need you to wake up, God, please wake her up."

CHAPTER 30

DIANELLA

*T*he sun glistens off the water waves as the sun sets on the horizon. It's a place that is peaceful in its own ways. It's a place to go after a long day of work or just a place where you can sit and think the best. It's a place where nothing else matters. Just the waves, the sand, and my thoughts.

The sand is seeping between my toes with every stride I take, water splashing on my legs, and I hear someone in the distance calling my name.

"Dianella!" they cry out. "Dianella!"

I turn to see who it is, and it's no other than Lenny Bradford. I can't believe my eyes, and for a moment, I'm lost between reality and make-believe. I close my eyes for a moment, and when I open them, he's standing before me, tall, handsome, strong, and firm. He's everything I've desired in a man and more.

"Hi, beautiful," he says with that deep, stern, seductive voice I crave so much.

"Hi. I've missed you so much," I confess with tears burning the back of my eyelids.

"I know you have, and that's why I'm here. I wanted to speak to you before you go."

"Go? I'm not going anywhere."

He stares deep inside my eyes, almost as if he can see straight through me. I reach for him, but he grabs my wrist instead.

"You don't belong here, Dianella. You belong with Lamonte." I shake my head fiercely in complete denial.

"No, I want to stay here with you."

"You can't, and I'm only here to let you know you must forgive yourself. Me leaving was not your fault. I did what I did for me, not you. You must know that. I loved you with every being in my fiber, but my love was not enough."

"Yes, it was. It was," I cry out.

"I'm not your soul mate, Dianella. Lamonte is. You must allow yourself to love again. You must allow yourself to love him."

"No, please don't. I made a mistake. I don't want to break up. I want you," I find myself begging. I don't want him to die. He doesn't deserve to die. Not like this.

"I didn't die because you broke up with me. I died because of my past. I was a horrible person, and it's time for me to take responsibility. You're the reason I got my act together. You're the reason I'm even able to speak with you. It could have been a lot different. Hold on to that. You changed my life, and I am forever grateful, and that's why it's time for you to go and enjoy your life the way you should. Love him, cherish him, and always know without a doubt you are loved.

I stand here like a blubbery mess, snot running down my nose, tears staining my cheeks, and heartache ripping me apart once again. But, deep down, there's a serine feel, almost like a moment of peace rushing all over me, and I no longer feel heartache. I no longer feel betrayal or misfortune.

Lenny starts to back away, and I see this light behind him, piercing my eyes, and a moment later, I don't see him anymore. Instead, I see walls as white as snow. I hear beeping sounds as annoying as the tinge of pain I feel in my side.

I feel something holding my hand, and I try to move it. I look down and see someone's head lying on the edge of the bed. It's Lamonte. It's his hand I feel in mine.

I squeeze gently. There's something in my mouth, and I can't speak.

I squeeze again, but a little harder this time, and he looks up.

Those beautiful grey eyes filled with so much sorrow and sadness; it pains me to glance into them. I then see a shift in his gaze, and now they are filled with hope, relief, and thankfulness.

"Oh, God. Dianella. Thank God. Here, wait just a minute, sweetheart. Let me get the doctor." He slips his hand out of my grip, and I feel lost in this moment, completely empty. "Nurse Casey, she's awake! Please come," Lamonte cries out.

He then rushes to my side, taking my hand into his, and I feel a rush of overwhelming relief spread throughout my body, a feeling I can only describe as comfort, desire, and safety.

A nurse comes in soon after, and she's such a breath of fresh air, so sweet and calm. The direct opposite of Lamonte right now. I can feel him shivering in my grip, and I try to squeeze a little more to give him comfort.

The nurse puts gloves on and then approaches me when the doctor walks in.

"Dianella, nod if you can hear me," the doctor instructs.

I nod my head.

"Okay. We are going to take the tube out of your mouth. You will need to remain still and cough as we pull it out. Okay?" the doctor instructs.

I nod once.

"Okay, here we go." She then pulls the tube out, and I cough. It fucking hurts, and my mouth feels like sandpaper and cotton balls.

The nurse holds a cup of water with a straw. She instructs me to take a sip. I drink so hard and so long, desperate for more.

"Take your time. You will make yourself throw up," the nurse tells me. I then release the straw and lay back.

"Do you remember why you are here," the doctor asks. "Take your time. There is no rush," she assures me.

I try to speak, but nothing comes out. I clear my throat once again to urge my speech, "Uh," is all I can muster at this moment.

I motion for a pen and paper or notepad. Nurse Casey hands me a pen and pad.

I write *I remember everything!*

"That's wonderful news!" the doctor announces. "Are you in any pain?" she asks.

No! I jot down.

"Your blood pressure is doing well, and your heart rate is steady. I want you to stay a couple more days, but for now, get some rest before we go over your injuries and what you need for recovery. Okay?"

Yes ma'am!

The doctor walks out along with Nurse Casey, and I turn toward Lamonte, who has been very quiet throughout the whole conversation.

I reach out for his hand, and he hesitantly moves, but he places his hand in mine. He avoids looking into my eyes, glancing at everything else but me. I see an overwhelming amount of emotions blazing through his demeanor. He's confused but grateful; he's terrified but wilful; he's broken but hopeful. He's feeling everything in this moment and doesn't know how to react to my recovery.

I slip my hand from his and write on the notepad,

Please look at me.

I hand him the notepad, and tears well up in his eyes. Finally, a sob escapes him, and his lips break apart slightly.

He drops his gaze to mine like it's the worst and most challenging thing he has ever had to do. And he breaks down into a puddle on the side of my bed. I do everything I can to comfort him like he has done so many times for me. I reach down and run my fingers through his soft curls, caressing and giving him what I can.

He needs me more than I need him, and I will damn well give it to him. After a while, he wraps his arms around my waist, and I have to say, they must have me on some good drugs because I don't feel a thing.

He pulls his arms from around me so quickly as if he forgot that he may hurt me, "Shit, I forgot. I'm so sorry. I'm such an idiot." I wave my hands and shake my head, letting him know he didn't hurt me. "I know, baby, but I know better. I've just waited for this moment for a long time."

I pick up the pen and paper. *How long has it been?*

"Six weeks, four days, and five miserable hours."

Wow!

"Yeah, tell me about it. It has definitely been a roller coaster."

Where is Jason? I have to talk with him.

"Shit, I was so happy you opened your eyes; I forgot to call every-one," he confesses. "Here, I will call him now."

He answers on the first ring. I've always liked that about my brother. If he didn't answer, I knew something was wrong.

"Hey man, Dianella just woke up. She wants to see you."

"Uh, hun," Lamonte says in the receiver. "She can't talk, but she can write…. Okay, see you soon, man."

"Jason, Lily, Amelia, Ryan, Kimberly, and Bradley are on their way. They've been here every day checking on you. Making sure you were comfortable and making sure I ate and bathed."

You've been here the whole time? I write.

"Yes, of course. I would never leave your side. Never."

I can tell he genuinely cares about me. It really shows, and if I didn't know any better, he might just love me.

Thank you, tears streaming down my cheeks.

"No, thank you, necessary," he cups my cheek, and for a moment, I think he's going to kiss me, but he changes his mind. Like, he's waiting for permission, or he's doing something wrong.

The door opens, and Amelia, Lily, and Kim rush at full speed, ahead.

"Oh, my gosh, Hunny. You had us scared to death. Shit, don't do that again," Kim demands.

"Yeah, you scared the hell out of us," Amelia admits.

"You even brought this big guy to his knees. Literally," Kim spits out, embarrassing Lamonte. I can see his cheeks redden on his pale face.

"Stop," Lily snaps. "Give the poor girl time to think, hell breathe."

"Time, she's been dicking off while we've been worried sick. It's time to get your ass up," Kim chastises.

And I burst out laughing without one sound coming from my lips. Shit, what the fuck is wrong with me? I shrug my shoulders.

"Give it time. You had the tube in your throat, and it might have bruised your vocal cords. You need to sip on some warm tea and lemon," Amelia says.

I nod my head in agreement.

I write on my notepad, *Where's Jason?*

"Oh, he's speaking with the officer posted at the door and the doctor."

Officer? I question.

"I didn't tell her," Lamonte speaks from the corner giving my family time with me.

"Oh, I see," Lily acknowledge.

What? I write.

"We will let Jason and Kim explain everything," Lily suggests.

I wait for what seems forever. What the fuck is going on? Why is everyone so apprehensive about letting me know what's going on?

Jason walks into the room smoothly and with stern poise. He approaches my bed and sits on the edge with Kim on the other side of me. Jason takes my hand into his, and I scan between them both, waiting for someone to tell me what the hell is going on.

Jason speaks first, "Dianella sweetie, when you were on the Talmadge Bridge, you managed to fight off two teenage boys, and you tried to fight off your last attacker. You even shot him, which was damn good, might I add. Anyways, your last attacker was our father, Johnathan. You slowed him down, but you didn't kill him. He's still out there, and we haven't been able to find him."

"We've had around-the-clock protection on you and surveillance on all of his property. He's nowhere to be found, but don't you worry, we will find him," Kim promises.

I glance into Kim's eyes first, then Jason's, and then I look up and find Lamonte. I can see in his eyes that they are telling me the truth. That this is not a sick joke. My father is still alive, and he's probably after me, again.

Fuck!

CHAPTER 31

LAMONTE

The devastation washing over her destroyed me. It damn near brought me to my knees. The last thing Dianella wanted to hear was her father survived, and now he's in the wind.

There was no way Dianella was going back to her loft, and she refused to put Lily and the kids in danger, even though Lily could hold down her own, so I suggested she come back to my home.

I could see the wheels turning and the rebuttals being tossed around in that pretty head of hers, but Jason and I weren't taking no for an answer. I know I couldn't keep her safe the first go around, but the second... there will be no second.

I've had surveillance and motion sensors installed while camped out at the hospital. I replaced all the windows in the home with bullet-proof and shatter-resistant glass. All the bullet holes were covered in the house and furniture replaced.

I didn't have time to replace the paintings, as they were my own.

My parents came by a few times to check on my well-being, and my brother called a few times. My sister, Alexis, however, refuses to leave until she knows that I'm okay. She's staying at my home for now and was the one who completely remodeled my home. She says it's her passion, and she's finally decided that interior design will be her major. I have to give it to her; she did a remarkable job.

Dianella gets released from the hospital today, so I came home to make sure Connie and Alexis had everything done for her arrival, even though I knew they did. I'm just a nervous wreck and have no idea how she will respond to all the changes.

"Lamonte, we got it. Go get Dianella and bring her home," Alexis demands. We will ensure everything is taken care of here; now go."

"Yes, Lamonte, go. I've bought all her favorite things, changed the linen in her room, and ensured all her clothing was brought over from her loft. We got this. You just make sure she gets home safely," Connie instructs.

"Thanks, ladies. I don't know what I would do without your help."

"Oh, we know," Connie snickers.

And we all laugh, erasing the tension in the room.

"Okay, okay. I'm leaving. We will be home soon."

I pull into the hospital bay and just sit for what seems like forever. I'm not sure what to expect, but I need to make sure Dianella comes home with me.

I call the nurses' station to let them know I'm here.

"We will be right down," Nurse Casey confirms. She has been an angel, to say the least. Very patient with us and encouraging. I will have to do something for her and the doctor for everything they did these past six weeks.

I step out of the SUV and run around to open the passenger door for Dianella. Once the doors slide open, my breath is taken away all over again. This girl is driving me mad. Her emerald eyes take me in completely, and I find desire washing over her immediately. Her lips part and she shakes her head as if she's debating if she should be looking at me that way. She's fighting the desire, and I can't blame her; it's my fault she was in that God-forsaken place. The doctor tried to give her an update on her injuries, but she flat out refused to listen and told her to get out.

Now she's coming home with me, and I know it's the last thing she wants to do. And once again, I can't blame her.

Nurse Casey pushes the wheelchair forward, giving me a chance to assist Dianella into the SUV. But, of course, she doesn't want my help. Not a surprise, but I'm here, nevertheless.

She reaches up and places her hand on the door rest and the other on the headrest; she then lifts herself up but loses her balance and falls back into my arms.

I immediately feel the fire blazing across my skin, and it takes everything in me to hold on to her and keep myself steady on my feet.

"Here, I got you," I whisper in her ear. She then gives up and allows me to hoist her into the SUV. I turn around and silently thank Nurse Casey.

"Now, Dianella. You must do everything the doctor ordered to have a smooth recovery. If you need anything, please give me a call. I am always here to help out, even though you don't want it," she smiles.

Dianella rolls her eyes because she's still having trouble speaking. It's getting better, but not to her full potential. She then sits back and allows me to put on her seat belt. Probably because she's exhausted. She then places her bag of clothes and meds on the floorboard.

We head home in complete silence. Once I pull up in the garage, she motions toward the extra car in the driveway.

"My sister, Alexis, is staying with me for a while. She's been overseeing the renovations, and I thought it was best for her to stay," a complete lie, but whatever, I don't give a shit anymore. My sister basically bombarded me and demanded I let her stay, more so because she probably was worried to death about me.

She nods her head in acknowledgment and takes a deep breath. Shit, I forgot she's never met my sister, and now, after everything she's been through, she has to meet some of my family for the first time.

"Shit, I wasn't thinking. You never met my sister."

She waves her hand, shaking her head, letting me know it's not a big deal, but I think it's a load of crock. It is a big deal for me anyway. I've never allowed anyone to meet my family, especially a woman.

I help her out of the car and allow her to wrap her tiny arms around my waist, and I feel that electric current running through my veins once again. Jesus, every time she touches me, it ignites me and makes me forget my insecurities all over again.

I help her up the stairs and into the mud room. I then guide her to my brand-new sofa, rustic brown leather with a soothing feel. She sits down and takes a deep breath while melting into the soft fabric. She closes her eyes for a brief moment until my sister enters the room.

"Hi," she says, all bubbly and full of smiles. "I'm Alexis, and you must be Dianella. I've heard so many great things about you." Alexis takes Dianella's hand into hers, and she soothes her fingers with her touch. Dianella smiles at her and reaches to give her a hug. Alexis embraces her, and I almost break at the sentimental gesture between them both.

I didn't know how much I needed this moment until now, how much I needed my sister to like Dianella, and how much I needed Dianella to accept my family. This is everything to me, and in this moment, I know without a doubt that I love Dianella, and I will do everything in my power to get her back, to make everything right again.

CHAPTER 32

DIANELLA

"*Oh, God, please don't. Not my ass. Please.*"

"*Ah, yes, I love it when bitches beg.*"

Shit, please, God, take this pain away. Please let me feel anything else but this.

Please, God.

He pushes through my tightness, ripping me apart. Then, screaming at the top of my lungs, I slip into a state of darkness. Everything around me slithering away. The lights, the colors, the sounds, and the smells are gone like flipping a cartoon book of emptiness.

I feel so alone, so lost, so abandoned. How can God let this happen to me? How can anyone do this to their own daughter? I'm nothing to him. He hates me that much; he's willing to rape me, sell me, and then just what, get rid of me.

It feels like hours have passed, and he's still pumping his massive dick inside of my ass, depleting anything I ever had or wanted. My body slamming through the bed, my head banging on something I'm not even sure of anymore. I no longer feel pain but numbness drifting through my veins. My eyelids become heavy, and my heart rate has slowed to a simple flutter.

"No," I hear myself scream. I roll off something and hit the ground hard. "Fuck, that hurt." I hear myself say, and it dawns on me; that I have my voice back.

I lift myself off the ground and get to my feet. It's painful as hell but not as bad as a couple of weeks ago.

Hell, I'm just glad I got my voice back. My vocal cords must be healing, like the doc said.

I've been in such a depressing rut, I feel like shit with every move I make, but at least I can move on my own now and speak, for heaven's sake.

I go into the bathroom so I can pee. Then, I sit on the toilet and relieve myself.

It's been two weeks living with Lamonte, Alexis, and Ms. Connie, and I just want to scream. I hate being confined in this prison with nowhere to go or nothing to do. I'm an outgoing, independent woman. I'm not built to sit around and do nothing.

I hear a knock on the door, "Hold on. I will be out in just a minute," I project softly. Don't want to overdo it.

Whoever it is, waits patiently for me to finish peeing and freshen up. Then, finally, I walk, or more like wobble, my way outside the bathroom and see Lamonte sitting on the edge of the bed.

He looks so freaking good right now, with his face scruffy with a fluffy beard and his grey eyes piercing my soul. His body is breathtaking, so hard and defined. He has those sexy jeans with a white tee that enhances his biceps. I just want to run my fingers through his curls and melt in his embrace.

He stands quickly when he notices me staring at him. We both been on pins and needles, basically on the fucking edge about to fall over with neither one of us willing to catch the other.

I can't stand this tension between us, so I break the ice first.

"Hi!" is all I can muster because I'm such a coward.

"Hey, I heard something, so I came to see what it was. I hear you got your voice back. That's pleasant news," he says meekly.

"Yeah, I fell out of bed, but I'm okay," I say quickly before he gets worried. "That's when I discovered I have a voice again. Thank goodness. I don't know how much longer I could have gone."

"You never know how much you need something until it's gone," he says with such conviction in his tone, making me wonder if he means my voice or something different entirely.

"Yeah, you got that right," I whisper, still afraid to use my voice to its full potential.

We stand in front of each other with this awkward silence, killing me.

"Are you hungry? Connie made steak, potatoes, and veggies."

My stomach almost growls, immediately betraying me completely.

Asshole.

"I see that's a yes," he smirks a little, and I almost fall apart. I miss that dimple in his cheek so much. I miss the way he touches me and the way he feels inside of me. God, I feel a shiver run down my entire body, and he instantly notices the desire in my stance.

I see his hazy gaze taking me in, and he wants me as much as I want him, but he doesn't make a move. He's putting the ball in my court. He did this before. He wants me to make the first move.

So, I step forward, and I see his eyes shifting, his hands bawled up beside him, and sweat piercing through his glands.

I take one more step and am directly in front of him. I feel the tension between us, and I sware we can burn the house down with just our gazes.

I glide my fingertips down his massive arms and look directly into his eyes, and I say softly, "I want you."

And that's all it takes before I'm lifted into his arms, and he's devouring me with his lips.

He's nipping and tucking and tasting every part of my mouth. His hands are searching for anything and everything to grab onto. Finally, he places me on the bed and tears his lips from mine.

Jesus, I feel fucking lost without his touch, his smell, God, his masculine scent...shit. I've wanted this for so long.

He takes my oversized shirt off and looks down at my body. Then, his eyes shift to something else, not desire anymore, but remorse, torture, or something I can't quite put my finger on. He backs away and starts to shake his head violently.

"No, we can't do this. I can't hurt you anymore. I won't."

"What are you talking about," I question.

"This, you. I did this to you." He points his hands at me, my body, my bruises, and it all makes sense now. He's blaming himself for what happened to me. I was taken from his home under his watch, and he couldn't protect me like he promised.

Well, little did he know, I was going to leave that night anyways. He wouldn't have been able to protect me anyways. He must know that this is not his fault.

I lift up, and he backs further away from me. Shit, I'm about to lose him. I have to stop this now.

"This is not your fault. You didn't know this, but I was going to turn myself over to those thugs anyways that night. I wanted to make love to you for one last night before I left. But that girl showed up, and we argued, and then I received that text from Maggie, and then all hell broke loose. It wasn't until I was captured that I realized this was wrong. That I had to fight back, that I had to come back to you." I take a deep breath and bow, ashamed of what I've done. "You're the reason I'm still here, still alive. I held on to your image, your strength; hell, I even apologized to you for what was happening because you didn't deserve to be put through something like that.

Everything was taken from me, and it was Johnathan who took it, not you. So please, stop blaming yourself. If you want to blame someone, blame me. It was me he wanted all along anyway."

Lamonte stands with disbelief in his stare, anger in his demeanor, but also a hint of sorrow and despair. He's feeling so much and can't possibly express what he feels right now.

The next thing I know, he turns, opens the door, and walks the hell out, leaving me to sulk in self-pity.

CHAPTER 33

LAMONTE

I storm to my room, slam the door, and start breaking all kinds of shit. I am so fucking furious right now.

"She was planning to fucking leave anyways. How the fuck am I supposed to forgive that? I tried every waking moment to protect her, and she was willing to just say fuck it all to hell. What the fuck?" I holler, throwing shit every fucking where.

I hear a knock on the door.

"What!" I spit out.

"It's me, Alexis," she opens the door slowly. "I'm coming in."

"What do you want?"

"I'm here to talk to you, and you will listen whether you like it or not," she demands. My sister can be a piece of work sometimes, but she knows she has me wrapped around her little finger.

"Fine, what the fuck ever," I spit out, throwing my hands up. I walk over to my loveseat and plop down. "What do you have to say?"

"Well, for starters, you can get rid of the bass in your voice. You will respect me, okay?" she deadpans. "Second, what's going on? Why are you breaking shit and cursing? And why is Dianella crying in her room? She thinks I can't hear her through the water running, but I can. So, what's going on?"

"She was going to fucking leave anyway. She was just going to hand herself over to those psychos and fuck whatever I was trying to do to get her out of it."

"So, you're upset that she was going to offer herself, but they stepped in first and took her anyway?"

"I'm upset because she had no regard for me, for us."

"Oh, I see." She pauses a little to gather her thoughts, probably not to piss me off any more than I am. "What if you saw it her way?"

"What do you mean?"

"What if she thought she was protecting you, and that's why she was going to do what she was going to do?"

"But—"

Cutting me off, "No, hear me out." She raises her palm in front of my face. "I know it was fucked up what she did or didn't do, but deep down, I believe she was trying to protect you, your family, her family, and her business. Can you imagine being responsible for someone's death?"

"But—"

She cuts me off again, "In her eyes, she feels responsible and wants to make things right. Now, I'm not sure what happened to her while she was missing, but I can tell you, she's going through some fucked up shit right about now. She has nightmares every night." I look up at her in total disbelief. "Yeah, I hear her screams. I just don't say anything because she comes off as wanting to take care of herself. She doesn't want anyone worried about her, including you. And you have to respect that. You have to understand what she has endured her entire life. She doesn't need anyone bossing her around. She needs someone to be by her side. It took a lot of strength for her to open up to you and you, sir, reacted very poorly. You must make this right, or you will lose her for good."

I place my face in the palm of my hands and feel my sister caressing my neck, soothing the tension in my muscles. Shit, I fucked up bad.

"What can I do to make it up," I ask more to God than my sister.

"You can start by apologizing and then listening and understanding her truth, then I suggest you do some serious graveling," she laughs. "Find out what's important to her and get it done."

"You're right. Thanks, sis." I give her a hug.

"And clean this shit up before I tell Connie what you did," she snickers to herself. "Come eat. I will get Dianella, but knowing her, she'll take her meal in her room. That's your chance," she winks at me.

I know just the thing to get back in her good graces, but first, I need to apologize and feed the woman I love more than breath itself.

CHAPTER 34

DIANELLA

I hear a knock at my door and yell, "Ms. Connie, I'm not hungry."

I lay in my bed with my back to the door, not really wanting to be bothered after that fucking debacle displayed earlier between Lamonte and me. He should be angry with me. I'm a fucking idiot.

I hear the door open, and fuck, what did I just fucking say.

I toss the covers back, ready to pounce, but it's not Ms. Connie; it's Lamonte.

"I thought you might be hungry, even though you say you're not."

"I'm really not in the mood. Please leave."

"I will leave, but I need you to hear me out first."

"Seriously, I know I fucked up. I don't need to hear from you that I fucked up. Trust me, I'm already beating myself enough without anyone's input. So, if that's what you're here to do, get the fuck out," I spit out, waving my hands for him to leave.

He places the food tray on the nightstand, and my stomach growls loudly, but I force myself to ignore it. Fucking belly betraying me with its fuckery.

He walks over to me with purpose in each step, with confidence oozing from his body. Finally, he stops in front of me, towering over me, forcing me to raise my gaze to meet his. I can feel the heat and tension radiating from his body. I feel so uncomfortable, but I try not to show any type of fear.

Fuck, I want him so bad, but I can't. I won't show desperation.

I then discover a cloudy storm shifting through his eyes, the grey hues battling each other for victory. His shoulders soften, and his once misty gaze shifts to lustful sin, and at that moment, I know he wants me. He needs me. He desires me.

He pierces through the walls I've erected and bulldozes his way into my shattered heart, picking up each piece at a time and putting it back together.

His gaze tells me so much, and I drink all of it. He steps back just a little, and I follow him. I want him to touch me. I want him to hold me. I want him to lift me up in his strong arms and have his way with me.

I reach for his arm, and he flinches a little. I need him to know that this is not his fault. The bruising on me is not his fault. What happened to me is not his fault.

"Please stop blaming yourself. I need you to understand, there was nothing you could have done." I place my palm on his cheek, allowing his fuzzy beard to give me the strength to project to him.

"I know...I...just, I don't know. I was to protect you. I had one fucking job, and I fucked that up. Look at you," he demands. He pushes me toward the mirror, forcing me to see what I've been avoiding for weeks.

I don't want to see the scars, bruises, pain, or heartache. Yet, I fucking live it over and over again every fucking night.

I shut my eyes tightly, refusing to look at that person in the mirror because that person in the mirror is not me.

"Please, baby, open your eyes. I need you to see what I see."

"No, I don't need to see what you see. I fucking play it live on repeat every fucking night," I spit out.

I back away from the mirror, sham clutching my soul all over again. I know he's right, but I don't want him to be right. I'm afraid of what I will see, what I will uncover.

"Please," is all he says, and my erected walls come crashing down all over again. My eyes burn with tears pouring. My heart aches with so much pain. And I feel bare. I feel completely open in this moment. I step forward, and I look into the mirror.

My first thought is this isn't me. This isn't my body, but then I take a closer look. I find my freckles on my cheeks and my birthmark on my left leg. I have bruises around my eyes with shades of purples, blacks, and blues. I glance at my arms, and there are slashes up and down my arms. My legs are colored with dreadful scarring, and the only thing I can manage to say is, "My God."

"Now, you see. Now you understand why it makes me so furious knowing that prick is still out there doing God knows what. For six weeks, I couldn't breathe, I couldn't think, I couldn't move from your side. I needed to know that you were safe and he could not get to you. And when you confessed that you would give yourself up to that type of torture broke me. I understand why, but I'm not happy about it. I'm fucking pissed because there is nothing I can do about it. I'm fucking pissed that this happened to you and not me. I'm fucking pissed that I can't take the pain from you. I can't take the memories away. I can't do anything, and it fucking pisses me the fuck off," he bellows wholeheartedly. "I want you so badly, but I'm afraid I may hurt you," he admits, throwing his face into the palm of his hands.

Once again, I reach for his arm, letting him know I'm here and understand completely. Like, I really understand.

"You will never hurt me, and if it does, I will let you know. I trust you wholeheartedly," I lift his head to glance into his eyes, searching for any type of connection and understanding. "I trust you, Lamonte." And then I pour my entire soul into the following words I speak, "I love you."

CHAPTER 35

LAMONTE

Those three simple words means more to me than she will ever know. The three simple words brought meaning to my life, bringing hope to my future, our future. They cure the aching pain in my heart, the damage piercing my soul.

Those three simple words mean the world to me. There is only one way to honor her strength in saying those three simple words. I must say them back.

"I love you too, Dianella." I take a small breath, giving her a moment to register what I just admitted. "You mean the world to me," is all I can muster up before she is in my arms, kissing me.

The softness of her lips collides with my very soul. She kisses me with such passion that I have no choice but to burst life into every touch, feeling, and movement we make. She will be my death, and if that's the cause of it all, I welcome it with open arms.

She tastes of salty sweetness covered in an orchid of apples. I slip my tongue between her lips and drink every ounce of her with absolute certainty that she's mine and only mine. I lift her in my arms and guide her to the bed. I place her down, taking her oversized shirt off as I release her. I stare down at her again, but I don't only see the scars surrounding her body but battle wounds from the war she fought all by herself.

I bend down and place a kiss over every scar, every stitch, every wound she's endured, letting her know I see her; whether she has blemishes or not, it's a part of her.

"You are so beautiful," I tell her with every fiber of my being. She needs to hear that I love her no matter what.

I take her nipple into my mouth and suck a little, feeling her body rise with anticipation. Tonight, I will take every second treasuring her body, my body.

Her body is my body, and I will claim it tonight.

I continue to suck and nip and pull on my nipples as I take my other hand and insert two fingers in my pussy. She openly moans at the intrusion and opens up even more for me. As I curve into her body, I feel her warm, soft walls close down on my fingers. She screams out my name as I feel hot moisture surround my fingers.

I abandon her nipples, desperate to taste her essence. I pull my fingers out and place them in my mouth, swirling her juices around my mouth.

"Oh my fucking God," she mummers under her breath. I smirk a little at her acknowledgment and dive right in with my tongue, exploring every inch of her pussy. I suck and nip, needing more than she can offer right now. I'm so fucking hard right now; I might just explode drinking her up. I manage to pull another orgasm out of her with just my tongue exploiting her inner soul.

I lift up, pushing my sweats and boxers down. Fuck.

"Baby, I'll be right back. I need to get a condom."

She wraps her legs around mine as I turn, preventing me from going. "I need you now, Lamonte. Please," she begs. Oh, for fucks sake. How the fuck do I deny her after that performance.

"Are you sure?" I ask, making sure she understands what she's asking.

"Absolutely. I want to feel all of you inside of me. I'm clean, and I'm on birth control. The doctor said my— uh, Jonathan didn't give me anything. I'm okay."

I know that had to be very hard for her to admit because we never talked about what actually happened to her, and I'm not going to ask now. "I'm clean too, baby. I just want to make sure this is okay with you."

"I'm more than okay. Now, fuck me before I fucking explode," and that's all the assurance I need before I enter into that tight fucking pussy of hers.

"Jesus," I bellow. It's been too fucking long since I've had her, and I'm pretty sure I'm not going to last long.

"Oh, my God, Lamonte," Dianella screams out. I thrust in and out, giving her all of me. She demands I go harder, but I might just die at this rate. I fucking can't get enough of her.

I thrust in her hard and firm as she grips my dick for dear life. "Please, harder. Please fuck the shit out of me!" and just like that, I give the woman I love more than anything in this world exactly what she wants.

I pound my dick inside her repeatedly, my balls slapping her ass, and just when I'm ready to explode, she fucking flips me over onto my back and rides my dick to new heights I didn't think was fucking possible.

"Holy shit!" I spit out. Her breast on display on top of me reminds me of the night in Charlotte, North Carolina. She fucking blew my mind away then, and she is fucking doing it again right now.

She rocks on top of me, swirling her hips, fucking the hell out of her dick. Yes, he's hers; she stole it from me long ago.

"Goddamnit, I'm about to come," she screams. I flip her back onto the bed and give her what she wants, a fucking ride of a lifetime.

We both collide, releasing our seed into each other, and I have to say, that was the best fucking experience I ever had, and it was with the woman I love more than life itself.

CHAPTER 36

DIANELLA

$\mathcal{I}$t's been three months since I left the hospital. I'm walking a lot better. My bruising has disappeared, well, except for the scarring. Unfortunately, that's there for life.

I'm in the car with Lamonte, heading somewhere he wouldn't tell me. He says it's a surprise. Every day, he has something or has gotten me something, which he doesn't have to do, but I stopped arguing a while ago. Our relationship has really grown over the three months, and I've never been happier.

His sister, Alexis, went back to school, so we have the house to ourselves. And I can definitely say we've put some good use to it. I mean, I can't keep my hands off Lamonte, and he sure as hell couldn't keep his hands off me.

Johnathan still has yet to cross my path, but I know he's lurking somewhere, just waiting to make his grand appearance. I know he's not done with me. Not by a long shot.

We pull up in front of my café, and I am blown away. It's no longer the dilapidated shit hole I left months ago. Instead, it's the direct opposite.

There are large bay windows that give an inviting feel to the place. The black iron rod seating outside upholds the industrial feel surrounding the outside area. Once you walk in, though, it's fairly modern yet chic. There's leather seating strategically placed at each small round rustic wooden table. Tall rustic black iron stools at the counter wrapped around the café give even more seating than before. Once you approach the front counter, glass cabinets house all the desserts and pastries. There is a state-of-the-art espresso machine on the back counter, with brand new coffee pots and makers.

Lamonte is holding my hand while I absorb every aspect of the café. "Did you do all of this?" I ask, tears filling my eyes.

"I had help from your brother and sisters and friends and some of my buddies from work. They all heard what happened and when I told them what I wanted to do, they pitched in with no problem," he explains.

"So, everyone did this for me?"

"Yes, Love," he stops us from moving forward and spins me around to face him. "You have so many people who love and care about you. They all know how much you love this place, and we wanted to do something for you that we all knew you would love."

I feel tears threatening to slide down my face, but I don't care right now. This is the single most precious thing someone has ever done for me. I place my palms on his fuzzy beard, bringing his lip to mine and making out like a schoolgirl in the middle of my café.

"Uhheem," I hear someone clearing their throat, causing me to jump a little.

I turn around and Lamonte straightens up. And then everyone starts bursting out laughing.

It's my sisters, brothers, and friends.

"We see you don't need anything from us at the moment," Kim announces.

"Yeah, she had his entire tongue in her throat," Lily laughs.

"Whatever, guys. I can kiss my man if I want to."

"She sure can," Lamonte agrees. And places another on my neck. Then, finally, he wraps his arms around my waist and pulls me back into his lap.

"See, my baby agrees. Now, back off," I tease.

"Leave the poor girl alone," Ryan defends me. Kim slaps him on the arm.

"You're supposed to have my back," she pouts.

"I do, Hunny. Shit, I'm going to have to make up for that one."

"You sure will," Kim teases.

"You guys, this is absolutely amazing. I love the café. It's gorgeous," I openly gush in front of everyone.

"Sweetie, you deserve the world if we could give it," Maggie states. "You saved me. You stopped those men from hurting me, and I owe you everything. So when Lamonte came to me about what he wanted to do, I jumped at the bit.

"I don't know what to say. I guess I didn't think of it that way. I just knew I had to get them from you. I never wanted any of you to get hurt. I would do it again if I ever was put in the position." Maggie reaches for me and hugs me so tight like she never wants to let go.

"Love, we have more to show you."

I pull away from Maggie, "There's more? You've done so much already."

"Like Maggie said, you deserve the world, Love."

I love the new nickname Lamonte has given me. Ever since I told him I loved him, he calls me Love. It makes me all giddy inside.

He takes my hand and guides me into the kitchen, and I'm blown away all over again.

173

"This is just too much. How on earth?"

"You deserve the best, and we can afford it."

"We?"

"Yes, Love, we." He tugs on my hand and guides me upstairs, with everyone following behind. "There's more."

"I don't know how much excitement I can take in one day."

"Well, you're in for so much more." Finally, we reach my loft, and he opens the door, pulling me along. I walk in and immediately fall to my knees, crying like crazy.

There's a banner draped across the living room that says in bold letter, "WILL YOU MARRY ME?"

Lamonte bends down and has a small box in his hand. He holds me patiently, allowing me to cry it out because I'm overwhelmed with joy.

"Love, sweetheart, will you make me the happiest man on earth?"

With tears blinding my sight, I reach to wrap my arms around his neck, crying even more than before. He lifts me off the ground, and I wrap my legs around his waist. My family and friends yell behind me, making me even more overwhelmed with joy. I whisper in his ear, "Yes, of course, I will."

He spins me around, smashes his firm lips to mine, and kisses me passionately.

I hear cheers and praises, and I never want this moment to end. "I love you so much, Lamonte."

"I love you too, Dianella. With all my heart and soul."

∼

Kim called, saying she had some stuff to talk to me, Jason and Lamonte about. It's probably about Johnathan, so Lamonte told everyone to come to our home.

Wow, our home. Who would have thought it? Me engaged. I had no desire to be with someone after Lenny, but Lamonte was a force to be reckoned with. He blew through my soul, intertwined his way into my life, and forced me to see what I would be missing if I let him go.

Connie moved all my stuff into his room, of course, because he said I was too far away from him.

I hear the alarm going off, letting me know someone is approaching the backdoor. Lamonte installed all of this fancy equipment to make me feel safe, especially now that he will return to work.

I speak on the intercom, letting Kim know I will be right down.

"Hey, Kim."

"Hey, baby girl. How's engagement life?"

"Spectacular. The sex is incredible, and the man that comes with it is breathtaking."

"Gross, don't nobody want to hear about his sister fucking a dude," Jason announces behind Kim.

"Well, close your damn ears because there is plenty of fucking in here." Jason makes a gagging noise.

"Oh, stop it," Lily slaps his arm.

"Ouch," Jason rubs his arm. "That hurt."

"Well, stop teasing your sister, and I wouldn't have to slap your arm," she teases. "You're just like the kids. They are three, and I swear Jason acts just like them."

"Well, you definitely have your hands full with this one; I can only imagine the kids tagging along," Kim states.

"Here, come in," I offer.

Everyone piles in the living room when Lamonte comes down the stairs.

"Hey, what's up, everyone," he plants a kiss on my lips, sending butterflies down my spine.

"So, I think I've found y'all, sperm donor," Kim spits out. No remorse in her tone at all. Gotta love her.

"Where is he?" Jason asks, apparently very impatient and not really with the shits with Kim right now.

"I was getting to that. I think he's still here. In Savannah!"

"What. The. Fuck!" I spit out. Totally in misbelief. "What the fuck is he still doing here? What does he want?" I question. I feel Lamonte grab my hand, trying his best to give me support.

"I honestly don't know, sweetie. My best guess is he's healing after the number you've done to him and is waiting for the opportunity to catch you alone," Kim says with genuine concern in her tone and demeanor. "You haven't been alone since you entered that hospital. He wants you to become complacent, and then that's when he will make his move."

"And she won't be until we find that prick," Lamonte bellows.

"Actually, Kim makes a good point. He won't grace us with his presence unless I'm alone. So why not make it so I am alone and then pounce?" I suggest.

"Over my fucking body," Lamonte and Jason shout in unison.

"But—"

"No!" Lamonte demands with such finality. And I don't bother bringing it back up. He has become so protective over me, but if I don't offer myself, I will spend the rest of my life looking over my shoulder. I can't do that. I won't do that.

CHAPTER 37

LAMONTE

I wake up to my dick being sucked by Dianella, and oh my fucking God, she is a fucking pro at dick sucking.

I'm on the brink of coming when she releases my dick and climb on top of me, shoving my dick inside of her, and fuck me until I explode.

"Fuck!" I holler. Hell, the only thing I can manage to spit out. Dianella has been a gift from God, and I would be foolish to let her go. After she brought me to my knees, literally, I take her pussy in my mouth, swirling my tongue all around her clit. She tastes so fucking good; I can have her for breakfast every fucking morning.

She shoves her small delicate hands into my hair, pushing my head further into her, begging me to give her more.

"Please, Baby, I need you inside of me," she pleads for the second time.

I refuse her request because it's my turn to bring her to her knees. I continue sucking and nipping when I shove two fingers inside her, bringing her ecstasy to full strength. She moans loudly, giving me every drop of her cum. I drink her up, not wanting to end this seduction.

She begs for my dick a third time, and I finally oblige her request. I fill her completely with myself, and she feels so good. I can't get enough of her. I need so much more, thrusting in her harder than ever. I make her scream my name with pure satisfaction in every syllable she utters.

"Lamonte, please!" she begs.

"Please, what, Love?" making her tell me what she wants.

"Please don't stop. I need...I want you. Baby, please harder."

Hell, I'm not sure I can go any harder than I am now, but I take it to another gear, slamming her into the mattress with every thrust, causing my dick to twitch inside of her, wanting to explode so fucking bad at this point. But I hold on just a little longer until I feel her nails digging into my back, causing me to empty every bit of me inside of her.

"Fuck, Dianella. Jesus fucking Christ!"

"Yes! Yes! Yes!" she screams out, and I collapse, managing to hold my dead weight without crushing her.

I roll over and bring her into my arms, kissing the nape of her neck. "That was fucking awesome," I whisper in her ear.

"It sure was. I can't get enough of you. I feel like a horny schoolgirl all over again."

"And you should. My little schoolgirl." She runs her fingertip across my arms, falling into deep thought. "What's on your mind?" I ask, knowing damn well what she's thinking about.

"Just us and how we've come so far. I remember trying to convince myself not to even think of you because I thought it would betray Lenny somehow. I was so torn for so long," she admits.

"I could never replace what you've had with Lenny. I wouldn't want someone to do it with me. But do know, I will love you with every fiber in my being. You're everything to me. Okay?"

She nods, "I know, and I realize that more and more every day." She turns in my arms, facing me. "I love you, Lamonte, and do know that I will do everything in my power to protect you, love you, and be by your side." Dianella gives me a soft and nurturing kiss, almost like it will be the last kiss she will ever give me, with yearning and need.

I place my palm on her cheek, bringing her closer. I slip my tongue between her lips, tasting her and absorbing everything she has to give to me. My dick awakens, and just like that, I'm rolling her over on her back, sliding through her tightness, making love to her nice, slow, and purposeful.

I roll over, reaching for Dianella, but it's nice and cold where she should be. I open my eyes, and it's still dark outside.

"Shit, what time is it?" I grab my phone off the nightstand, and it's a little after four in the morning.

I get out of bed and head to the bathroom. I've got to piss.

After freshening up, I head downstairs to find Dianella. She's not in the gym or the office. I check the kitchen because that's where I usually find her, baking something. Once I make it to the kitchen, I see that all the lights are off, and the alarm is still set.

"Dianella," I yell throughout the house, wondering where the hell she could be.

I have a terrible fucking feeling about all of this. So, I head back upstairs, get my phone, and check the cameras.

Around two in the morning, I see Dianella heading out the garage in the SUV I bought for her, "Fuck, where the hell could she be going this late at night?"

I dial her number, and it goes straight to voicemail. "Fuck."

I dial Jason.

"Hello?" he answers, all groggy.

"Hey man, Dianella is gone. She took the SUV, and her phone is going straight to voicemail. I think she went after Johnathan," I yell in the phone. "Man, she fucking gone."

CHAPTER 38

DIANELLA

I'm headed to my loft in the middle of the night. I know he will be waiting for me there. Johnathan has no problem attacking me when I'm alone, so why not give him what he wants and get this shit over with?

I pull up in the lane and enter through the backdoor. I know Lamonte will track the vehicle and hopefully save me from gutting my dear old daddy from neck to navel.

I head for the knife drawer and pull out a box cutter. I take the blade out and slide it in between my French braid. I sit on a stool in the dark, waiting for his sorry ass to show the fuck up.

A few minutes pass by, and I hear the backdoor click.

Game on.

I watch as I see a tall figure slowly creeping through the kitchen and heading upstairs. I wait to see if anyone else follows, and I'm sure he's alone; I follow behind him. He makes his way up the stairs, and before he can close the door, I kick it in, causing him to stumble over.

"Hello, daddy!" I spit with sarcasm dripping from my tone. "It's strange meeting you here, in my loft, in the middle of the fucking night."

"I can say the same about you, my dear," clearly caught off guard.

He straightens himself up, gripping the table a little. Seems he's still hurt or wants me to believe he's hurt.

"What do you want?"

"I want you, darling."

"Well, you can't have me, so leave."

"Now, why would I do that? I've waited months for this moment."

"So. Have. I," I stare him down with confidence and anger oozing from my pores.

Pissing him off, he comes charging at me like an angry bear. I throat punch him, and he bellows over, clutching his neck for dear life. I then kick him in his ass, forcing him to fall to the ground.

I turn around and stomp on his head, causing it to bounce off the ground. I keep plodding until he grabs my foot and flips me on my back. He climbs on top of me, trying to put his hands around my throat, but he can't get a grip. I greased my skin with Vaseline, making it very difficult for him to hold on. Finally, I knock his arms out of the way with my elbows, and he punches me in the side.

It hurts like hell, but I show no signs of pain or fear. I'm able to push him down with my elbows on his knees and pop my hip up to throw him off me. He grabs my shirt, ripping it off completely. He sticks his hands down my pants and inserts his fingers in my vagina. I let him. I want him to think he's got me where he wants me.

He thinks he's pleasuring, and I allow him. I stop fighting altogether. I allow him to roll me on my back and let him take my tights off. He then slides his pants down and inserts his dick inside of me. I pretend I'm scared to death, and the moment he begins to enjoy himself, I pull the razor blade out of my hair, cutting some off completely. I wait for the moment I know he has reached his climax, which isn't long at all. I take the blade and slice his throat completely open while he's ejaculating inside me. I watch the blood drain from his wound, splashing on my face and around my body, I'm finding closure and complete satisfaction in watching the life slip away from his useless body.

He collapses on top of me and I manage to push him off of me, letting his body roll onto the floor. I hear his gasping for any type of air he can manage to capture. And as his eyes widen with horror and disbelief, I take the blade, cut his dick off and let him watch me throw it in the fucking garbage disposal while his eyes roll to the back of his fucking head.

I walk out of the loft, leaving him on the fucking floor, and head down the stairs, running directly into Lamonte and Jason, "Fuck, Dianella. What the fuck happened? Where the fuck are your clothes? Who's fucking blood is this? Where is Johnathan?" they both spit out in droves.

All I can muster to do is point and collapse in Lamonte's arms before I black out entirely from pure exhaustion. Finally, the satisfaction, I've been searching for.

Finally!

～

I wake up in the hospital once again, but I don't have tubes in my throat, and Lamonte is nowhere to be found.

I try sitting up, but I'm a little lightheaded. I hear voices outside my door, but I can't determine who they are.

I push the call button on the side of the bed, and the door opens after a few minutes.

"Hi sweetie, how do you feel?" Lily asks.

"My head hurts a little and my side, but other than that, I'm fine. Where's Lamonte?"

I see sorrow in her eyes briefly, but it disappears just as quickly as it appeared.

"Um, sweetie, he had to leave."

"Will he be back?"

"I'm not sure. He said he couldn't see you like this again, not ever. I tried talking to him, but he wasn't hearing me. I think this was too much for him. Give him time; he will come around."

"So, he's not coming back?" I ask, totally terrified of the answer.

"I would give him a day or two. Then give him a call. In the meantime, you can stay with us. You know we have the room."

"No, I need to talk to him now. He has to understand why I did what I did."

"He knows. He's just hurt right now."

"I know, and that's why I have to go to him." So I try to get out of bed this time, and she pushes me back.

"Dianella, please. You've been through a lot. I need you to take it easy."

"I can't. I can't lose him. I need him. I did all of this for him, for us."

"I know, sweetie. I know."

Tears flooding down my face, streaming in puddles, as I'm completely losing it in front of Lily, and she cradles me in her arms, trying to soothe and comfort me, but the only person I want right now is Lamonte.

CHAPTER 39

LAMONTE

I can't right now. I just can't deal with this shit, not again. What the fuck was she thinking? He could have killed her. He could have done…fuck, I can't even think about this shit. I can't think about the shit he did to her. God, what was she thinking?

I made sure she got to the hospital safely, but there was no fucking way I could stay there and watch her go through that same shit, not again.

I fucking left her there. Shit, I left my fiancé at the fucking hospital by herself. Fuck, I said I would never hurt her, but she fucking destroyed me without a care in the world for a second time. How could she disregard me so easily?

I fucking gave her a ring for fuck's sake and devoted my entire being to her and she go and put herself in danger like this?

I've pretty much burned a path in the wooden floor, pacing back and forth trying to understand this shit.

I head to my liquor cellar and grab a bottle of Don Julio 1942. I need a fucking drink. That's the only way I can drown my fucking misery.

I pour me a glass and chug it down, letting the soothing burn slide down my throat. I pour another and take it back again.

Fuck this shit, I pour another and take the bottle with me to the balcony, prepared to fucking drink myself into oblivion.

~

"Get up!" I feel someone pushing on my arm. "Get up, Lamonte."

I open my eyes and the bright light pierce through my rectal, causing me to close them again. "Fuck, turn the fucking lights off!" I demand.

"That's not the light asshole, it's the sun. You're outside passed the hell out," Alexis spits out. "What the fuck is going on?"

"Nothing, why are you here?"

"Connie called. She said she tried everything to get you up and you wouldn't budge. She was going to call the police, but then realized you were fucking drunk off your ass."

"Connie needs to mind her own business. I'm fine."

"No, you're not. The last time I've saw you like this, you and dad got into it. Now, you're going to get your ass up and tell me what's going on. Where's Dianella?"

"Fuck her!" I spit out.

"Well, now I know its about her. What happened?"

"She fucking…she fucking…" is all I can spit out before I vomit all over the place and fucking cry my worthless heart out.

Alexis soothes my back, but also throws little fucking shots at me for being so fucking stupid. "This is why you shouldn't get pissy drunk. Connie is making you her special hangover cocktail."

"How do you know about her special cocktails," I challenge.

"I'm not that little girl pissing you off anymore."

"No, you're a pain in my ass," I spit out.

"Whatever."

Connie walks on the balcony hands me her special cocktail. "Here Lamonte, drink all of it, now," Connie demands.

I grab the glass and chug it down with a swift swallow. "Fuck, that's gross."

"Serves you right. Now sit the fuck up and tell me what's going on. I'm not leaving until you do."

"She fucking went to him. She fucking went to him and killed him like the fucking dog he is," I spit out, slurring my words.

"And how is that wrong?" Alexis asks as Connie leaves, closing the sliding door behind her.

"Because, damnit."

"Because—"

"Because I specifically told her not to go. Not to put herself in danger. And she did it anyway. She did it any fucking way. How could she? He could have killed her," I demand.

"Ah, I see now. You couldn't protect her again, and you couldn't stop her from risking her life, yet again, to protect the people she loved and cared about."

"Yeah...what—no, she...no damnit...she should have waited for me, for anyone. She did all of this and never once told me she was going to."

"She didn't tell you because she knew you were going to stop her. She knew that the only way she could get that son of a bitch was to do it alone. You can't possibly fault her for that. Yeah, it was incredibly stupid of her to go alone, but maybe she had no other choice. Didn't you say her sister-in-law and friend experienced the same thing? What did they do?"

"Fuck—I didn't think about that. They did the same fucking thing."

"Yeah, she comes from a line of strong women. They get shit done and do it without getting their family hurt or killed in the process. They are willing to sacrifice themselves before they let anything happen to the people they love. Look, Lamonte, she needs you. You're afraid she doesn't need you, but she does, just in a different way. She needs you to support her through this shit, because without your support, she will absolutely fall apart."

"I don't know if I can handle that. I don't know if I can watch the woman, I love put her life in danger every day."

"Are you serious right now? Like seriously, dude, you put yourself on the line every fucking day you put that uniform on and you expect her to be okay with that? Why can't you do the same for her? The hypocrisy of it all. At its highest level, if you ask me."

"Fuck!" shoving my head in my hands. "I did it again, didn't I? I'm such an idiot."

"No, you're not. You just needed to hear it in a different perspective. You need to sit down with her and let her tell you everything. And even though it won't be nothing you want to hear; you must hear her story. That is the only way you will understand why she does the stuff that she does. If you don't, you will lose her, sooner than later. I'm pretty sure I said this same shit before. Get your head out of your ass and go get your girl!"

CHAPTER 40

DIANELLA

*N*ever-ending tears stained my cheeks, heart-wrenching pain twisted my gut in two, and fear overwhelmed me completely.

I've done it again. I hurt the man I love, and now he's gone. How do I experience two great love stories in one lifetime and lose them both? How?

It's been two long miserable weeks of laying in my bed, eating butter pecan ice cream, and crying at every little memory I have of him, and I still haven't heard from Lamonte. I really messed up.

I'm back at my loft because the last thing I wanted was to be bothered by my brother's over-protectiveness and my sister's overwhelming affection. Don't get me wrong, I love them wholeheartedly. I just want to wallow in self-pity for an eternity. I don't deserve Lamonte. I don't deserve to be happy.

I hear a knock at the door, but I don't give a shit. As a matter of fact, I can't remember the last time I got up to eat or drink or just brush my damn teeth. I don't care anymore.

I hear another knock and continue to ignore it like it's a figment of my imagination.

Maggie has been running the day-to-day things downstairs, so there is no reason for me to move a fucking muscle.

I then hear voices. Fuck my life. I just want to be left the fuck alone. That's all I ask.

"Dianella," I hear Lily and Amelia's voices. Then I hear a gasp. They must've found the crime scene I never bothered to clean up. What's the point? It reminds me every day of the shit I put Lamonte through and the very reason why I did what I did.

My father would have stalked me, tortured me, and then killed me for his own fucking pleasure. I had to beat him at his own fucking game. I had to. Such a useless son of a bitch. To do such things to your own daughter is the sickest thing a person could do. He deserved to die and so much more.

They finally make it to my bedroom, and I still don't move a muscle.

"Oh, Dianella," I feel one of them rushing to my side. "Baby girl, we need you to get up."

I don't say a thing.

"Get up, Dianella," Kim demands. Well, yep, the whole fucking crew is here.

"What do y'all want?" I question with disdain in my tone. I really don't feel like this shit right now.

"We want you to get the hell up. You've been wallowing in your shit for two weeks. It's time to get the fuck up, and I mean now!" Kim demands.

"No!" I spit out.

Kim snatches the covers off me, and I fucking lose it.

"What the hell!" Lily holds one arm down, and Amelia has the other. Finally, Kim climbs on top of me and slaps the shit out of me. I mean, it stung so bad. "Ouch, please, just leave me alone," crying to myself.

"We can't do that, Dianella. You mean more to us than you will ever know. We love you, Di. We can't sit back and watch you slip into depression like this. You are so much stronger than this."

"No, I'm not," I finally admit. "I fucked up. I lost him, and he hates me," I cry out. "It hurts so much. I just want the pain to go away. Please take the pain away," I beg. "Please."

"You have to start by forgiving yourself. I know exactly what you're going through. Hell, we all do," Lily admits. "You must be strong and be willing to accept help when you need it, and Hunny, you need it."

"You have so much going for you. Be the strong woman I know you can. The first step is forgiving yourself. The second is getting out of this bed," Kim suggests.

"Lamonte loves you, sweetie. He would have never proposed if he didn't."

"He would have never left if he did. He left me," I cry out. "He left me."

"He was scared. Can you imagine the love of your life risking it all, and there was nothing you could do about it? Can you?" Amelia demands.

I sit there because I don't have an answer to that question. I don't know what it feels like.

"Yeah, I thought so. He was a nervous wreck when you were in that hospital the first time. We had to make him take showers and eat because he was so afraid you would wake up, and he wasn't there by your side. And to have to go through that a second time would have destroyed him. Hell, it did. It took Jason, Ryan, and Bradley to hold him down. He was going to destroy everything in that hospital. He had to leave. He couldn't watch you suffer anymore," Amelia continues.

I sit in bed, absorbing everything they just said, crying hysterically.

"Oh, God!" is all I can muster before I start screaming at the top of my lungs. The pain I'm experiencing is unbearable. I can't take it anymore. I just can't. "He doesn't want to see me."

"How do you know? You haven't left this place in two weeks," Kim chastises.

Kim is the no-sugar-coating bitch of the group. She tells it like it is and makes you feel like shit afterward. But that's what I love about her. She will always keep it real.

"What if I go to him and he turns me away? I don't think I can handle that type of rejection right now," I admit.

"That's a chance you will have to take, sweetheart," Lily suggests.

"Now, what do you say?" Amelia holds her hand out to help me out of bed.

I look at it for a moment debating if this is something I actually can do. Is this something that I am brave enough to conquer? I've been in such an entangled debacle; it's time for me to get my shit together.

I place my hand in hers and let her lift me from the bed. "That's my girl."

"I have something to do first."

~

There is so much that has happened in the past couple of years, I don't even know where to start. But I do know one thing, I need my mother. I need her comfort, that bond that I crave so much. I was so young when I lost her, but I know she has always watched over me.

That's why it's imperative that I now pay my mother the respect she deserves. I owe her so much more and then some. I've been so selfish over the years, so mad, so hurt…but now, I have to release that hold over me.

I have to let it go.

I pulling up to Bonaventure Cemetery. The cemetery which became one of the most iconic landmarks in Savannah due to the featured novel in 1994, Midnight in the Garden of Good and Evil, by John Berendt, one of my favorite authors. I get out of the car and follow the map to her grave site. Once I find it, I immediately realize that I'm not the only one who's been here. I see fresh orchids placed and her tombstone free of debris.

Must be Jason.

I wonder why he never told me that he visits regularly. Maybe because I had to find my own way here. Having the knowledge of my depression when Big Mama passed, could hinder any person from trying to reach me.

As I approach, I feel a slight breeze, chilling my skin, causing goose bumps to form on my arms, forcing me to pull my oversized sweater across my shoulders.

"Hey mom," I manage to start. "Where to begin. Even as a child, I never understood women have secrets, and that some are told to their daughters, but you never got the chance. I never understood why your fate was chosen and never really given the opportunity to flourish, never having the opportunity to guide me, teach me, mold me in the woman you wanted me to become. No, you had to rely on Big Mama, and mom…I can say, she did a wonderful job. She even got Jason to be a strong young man. He has a beautiful wife and three gorgeous children."

I take a seat on the ground next to my mom's tombstone, tears streaming down my face, "I don't know what to do any more. I'm so scared," I cry out to no one in particular. "Did you know this was to be my fate? To have two great loves in one lifetime at such a young age? Did you know?" I demand.

With wind picking up, I watch the leaves dance in the breeze. I know I'll never get the answers I crave so dearly.

But, I do know one thing.

I have to go to him.

I have to get him back.

Lenny is right, Lamonte is my soulmate. I remember everything, every conversation, but what I really needed was my mom.

Mom, I know I can be the woman you want me to be. I have a successful business, friends, a family, and a man who loves me more than life.

I hurt him so much and I know if I want this tortured fate to end, I must be the strong woman I know I can be. It will be hard as hell and even scary, but I have to be strong enough to let the pain go and allow happiness into my heart. I can't be afraid anymore.

I stand with new purpose, new outlook on life. "Thanks mom. I love you more than you will ever know. I know you'll be proud of us. I know you will," I smile to myself.

I'm standing outside his door, terrified to even move an inch. All my doubts and fears are creeping back into my heart and squeezing the life out of me. I can't pass breath through my lungs, and I feel like I'm about to pass the hell out.

"Fuck, what am I doing?" I question between each labored breath. I prepare to turn around and get the hell out of here when the door opens. "Shit," I say under my breath.

"Dianella?" Lamonte says with such passion and strength. Something I don't have right now.

After what seems like forever, I turn to meet his gaze. He's in his full uniform, navy blue with gold accents, because he's a supervisor. He has his bulletproof vest on underneath, making him look even supe-rior in front of me. His command stance takes what little breath I have, causing me to part my lips even more.

He's clean-shaven, beard completely gone, and hair cut short; I can barely see his curls I love so much. I drink him in because this may be the last time I see him again.

I begin to turn and coward away when I feel his hand wrap around my wrist, causing electricity to shoot straight through me. "Please, wait. I really need to speak with you."

"Why?" I ask. "It's been two and a half weeks, and I've heard nothing from you," I spit out with anger I didn't think I had. He nudges just a little to encourage me to turn around, but I really don't want to.

"Dianella, please," he begs. I turn around with tears stinging the back of my eyelids and a colossal lump caught in my throat that I seem to can't pass on my own.

He wraps his arms around me, comforting me, being my rock. Finally, I can't hold the tears back anymore, allowing them to spill over. I break and have no strength to stand on my own. He swoops me into his arms and carries me into his home. He sits on the sofa with me in his lap, cradles me, and rocks me back and forth, giving me time to breathe on my own once again.

I have no idea how long we sit here before I raise myself entirely on my own. I need to be strong. I need to tell him how I really feel. He needs to know the truth about everything.

"Lamonte, I came over for a reason. You need to hear the truth about everything. You need to understand why I did what I did, and then I will leave the decision to you whether you want to be with me again or not."

He nods his head, urging me to continue. I'm nervous as shit, but I have to find the strength that I clearly don't have. Here goes nothing.

"Apparently, my story starts long before I even arrived on this earth. As you know, my father was the leader of a gang that sells drugs and women. He wanted my mother to be a part of this organization, and when she refused, he had her raped and beaten. He told her that her job was to have girls and groom them for his collection, but her first child was a boy, Jason. He decided to groom Jason into his right-hand man, but my mother got pregnant with me. His focus shifted back to selling his offspring to the highest bidder, and my mother couldn't allow that," tears forming in my eyes once again and my hands trembling with fear. I continue. "So, she gave us to her guardian, Big Mama. You see, my father knew my mother was an orphan, but she never spoke about her guardian who raised her. This is how we were able to grow up with such a different life. He later killed her by giving her drugs and forcing an overdose upon her. Big Mama never told us the true story because she knew Jason would track that asshole down and kill him. Jason was out of control when our mother gave us up. He didn't understand why, so we pictured her as a drug addict, so we would stay away."

Taking a deep breath, "So, when I grew up and met Lenny, I had no idea he was a part of a gang, let alone my father's gang. Lenny was killed because he betrayed his oath, but when my father found out who I was by coming into my café, he discovered a new interest in me. You see, he figured he could continue his plan by taking me and grooming me to be exactly what he wanted, a prostitute, a human slave. So, the night he took me and learned about Maggie, I had to stand up for myself. I had to fight back, knowing that he probably would kill me by doing so. I just needed him to leave Maggie and my family out of it. So, I offered myself to him. I offered to have sex with him in order to save Maggie. He accepted the offer, but little did I know, he wanted to rip me apart. He forced anal sex with him and so many other men and so many objects. I woke up with blood every-where. I was so scared, I had to get out of there. I didn't even notice all the other bruising. I just knew I had to go. So, I jumped out of a window, landed in bushes and ran across the field, hopped over a fence, and then stayed in the wood line so I could make it back home. But the bridge didn't have a wood line, so I took the chance of running across, but they found me. It was fight or flight at that moment. I honestly don't remember anything that happened on the bridge; I just remember waking up at the hospital."

I take another deep breath, and Lamonte continues to hold me for support. "When Kim and everyone else came over, and I mentioned offering myself, I wasn't doing it to betray you or anyone else. I was doing it to save all of you. You see, he told me he would torture my entire family if I didn't do as he said. I believed him. And when y'all told me that he wasn't dead, I knew I had to do something. So, I went to the one place he would find me alone, my loft. I waited for him to come through the back door, climb the stairs, and attack me. But he didn't realize that I was watching him the whole time. He didn't realize I had a box cutter hidden in my hair. He didn't realize that Jason taught me how to fight at all costs. He was too arrogant to realize that little ole' me was tougher than he thought, so I let him fuck me while I slit his throat and before he took his last fucking breath, I cut his dick off and threw it in the garbage disposal while he watched in horror. He will never hurt me or anyone else again. And that's all of it. The bitter truth of it all."

I take a deep breath and prepare to stand, but Lamonte pulls me back down. He wraps his arms around me and cries out, "I'm so sorry. God, I'm so sorry," he repeats over and over again.

"It's not your fault. It's none of our fault. This happened before us. It was up to one of us to finish it. That, someone, was me. You must know that I would do anything to protect the people I love. I've learned from the best, and if you can't handle that, I understand that we must go our separate ways. I just had to tell you the truth even though it was extremely hard to do."

"Dianella, please. Let me speak." I sit, waiting for my demise, for my unbearable torture to become a reality.

He pushes me forward and turns me around, forcing me to look into his eyes. I see the storm conflicting with sensitivity. I see a calmness blanketing across the grey hues, giving him strength in his gaze. His tears streaming down his firm cheeks contradicts his fear in his touch. There are so many emotions scattering in this one gaze it tears me into pieces. I did this to this robust and adventurous man. I broke him down, and now he doesn't want anything to do with me. I break our gaze first, not wanting to see the conflict in his eyes.

He places both palms on my tear-stained cheeks and lifts my face, forcing me to look back into his eyes. "I love you, Dianella. I'm not pushing you away. I'm not letting you go. You are my life, and I am nothing without you in it. I'm sorry for abandoning you when you needed me the most. I'm sorry it took so long for me to get my head out of my ass. I've been transitioning at work, and I've been allowing that to be my excuse for not going to you, and I'm sorry for that. Please forgive me?"

"You're asking me to forgive you?" I question with much astonishment in my tone. "You have no reason to ask for forgiveness. It's me who should be asking."

"No, I was a coward for leaving you at that hospital. I just...I just couldn't see you like that again. It nearly broke me the first time. I was so angry with you, but my sister, once again, told me how much of a fool I was for treating you like that." I make a mental note to thank Alexis. She really has been instrumental in keeping us together.

"Well, if it wasn't for my sisters digging me out of the rut I was in, this wouldn't be happening right now," I wavy my finger between the two of us. "We must thank our sisters for being our strength and kicking our asses. I know I needed it. They literally kicked my ass back to reality," I laugh mostly to myself.

"Tell me about it. Where do we go from here?" he asks hesitantly.

"Where do you want us to go? Like I said, the ball is in your court. You're the one that has to deal with all of my crazy shit, but hopefully, it's done. Johnathan is dead. Lenny is dead. Jason said the entire gang has been brought down by SIU."

"Yes, that's what I wanted to talk to you about. I've been moved to SIU. I'm the supervisor of the unit now. That's why I've been so busy. We took them down this past weekend. The whole crew."

I can't contain my excitement when I throw myself in Lamonte's arms, kissing him with such passion I didn't think I had. He returns my kiss and takes completely over like he's been wanting to do this the whole time.

He's licking, nipping, and tugging at my lips, lifting me up in his arms and gently placing me on the sofa. I watch him take his uniform off, piece by piece. First, his duty belt comes off, placing it on the floor next to us. He then zips his shirt down, revealing his vest underneath. Next, he lifts his vest over his head along with his white tee shirt. He displays such a strong body with abs that are so touchable right now, and all I want to do is lick them just to get a little taste of what I've been missing.

He goes to drop his pants, and oh my God! I fall to my knees, desperate to taste every inch of his magnificent dick. The veins pulsating, giving me the strength to take over his body. I need him so much right now.

I wrap my lips around his huge dick, feeling him shiver every inch I take. I lick and nibble just a little to stimulate every nerve he has. I bob back and forth while he moans and shoves his hands in my hair, pulling the long strands out of my messy bun.

He forces his dick down my throat, and I let him take everything from me because he deserves everything I have to offer. He deserves more than I have to offer, but if I can give him this, I shall. He pushes through my gag reflexes, and I let him. I suck as he pulls out, and I feel him swell in my mouth. I know he's about to come, and I welcome it. I want to taste him, drink from him as much as he wants to give to me. I stop him from pulling entirely out by tugging on his ass cheeks. I continue to bob back and forth, and before I know it, he explodes in my mouth, giving me all of his cum and then some. I lick and lap every drop before he pushes me back on the sofa, rips my panties completely off from under my dress, and thrusts his large, thick dick inside me.

It fucking hurts, but I don't give a shit. I welcome the pain. I need this more than life itself. I need all of him. I need to feel alive again.

He thrusts harder and harder, slamming me into the couch. He demands me not to move a muscle, raising my hands above my head, holding me down as if I'm trying to get away.

"Fuck, Dianella. I fucking needed this," he bellows through gritted teeth. He continues to ram inside of me, giving me a ride of a lifetime. "I don't want you fucking no one else. Do I make myself clear?" he demands through thrust.

Apparently, I don't respond quick enough because he repeats himself more firmly and aggressively. "This is my pussy. Not your fucking father's, not fucking Lenny's, mine, Goddamnit. Your pussy is mine," he assures me, but then I start to cry because I know now why he's so mad. I know now why he's so hurt. I fucked these other men, and there was nothing he could do about it.

"I'm so sorry, Lamonte. I wasn't thinking," I cry out. "I'm so sorry."

I feel him stop abruptly, causing me to open my eyes. The horrible fear he has in his eyes terrifies me. "Oh my God, Love, I didn't—" he tries to apologize, but I interrupt him.

"Please don't apologize. You didn't hurt me," I lie, trying to sound convincing. "I hurt you."

"But you don't deserve this. I'm taking my frustration out on you, and there's nothing acceptable about this. I should not be hurting you. I should be loving you," he cries out.

He throws his head back with such frustration.

I decide at this very moment that I have to fix this. I have to heal us. I climb onto his lap and straddle his legs. He jumps a little, but I settle him back down. I run my hand up and down his shaft to get him hard again. He's fighting me, but he's also enjoying this pleasure.

He moans after each stroke, growing within my grip, giving me life to my arousal. I need this as much as he does. I rub his tip against my lips, allowing the moisture from me to lubricate him. I then sit up a little and place his shaft at my entrance. I slowly settle down on his dick, allowing it to fill me completely. I stay put for just a moment giving us both a chance to adjust.

I then lift up and down, providing friction for both of us. I swirl my hips and make love to the man I love. I feel his breathing picking up and his hands gliding up and down my back. My head falls back because this feels so good to me.

Lamonte lifts my dress over my head, dropping it in a puddling heap with his uniform. I know he should be heading to work, but I don't care right now. My man needs me, and I will give him everything he needs and desires.

His soft moans give me energy to continue my pleasure. I rock harder and harder because I can't get enough of him. He then lifts to his feet, with my legs straddling him. He bends me back, bracing me with his arms. He slams his dick inside me repeatedly, causing me to explode with ecstasy. I come all over his dick, whimpering his name.

After several more strokes, I feel him swell inside of me and then explode, giving me all of his seed, filling me completely. He settles back down, taking me with him, and I collapse on his body with his dick still inside me.

We both drift away like we haven't slept in months, and it's the best way to go, in his massive yet gentle arms.

EPILOGUE

DIANELLA

SIX YEAR LATER

"Congratulation, Captain Wilson," I wrap my arms around Lamonte's neck and give him a kiss.

"Thank you, Love."

"Daddy, Daddy. You did it."

"Yes, I did with your help, baby girl." Lamonte gives our daughter, Dahlia, a kiss on the cheek as he picks her up in his arms. Dahlia is four now and has won the heart of everyone around her. Lamonte was promoted to Captain and will be in charge of Criminal Investigations, with Jason as his Lieutenant. Jason finally decided to go for the Sergeant's exam, and when the Lieutenant's position opened up, he put in for it.

After all the cases he, Lamonte, Lily, and Kim solved, they deserve these accommodations. Lily decided to leave the force entirely. She's now partners with Kim, who runs the largest women's shelter in the southeast. Amelia finally decided to become a nurse and now has her own practice. Ryan and Bradley are doing very well at their financial firm, and me, well, I have three more cafés across Savannah, with Maggie running one and Alexis, Lamonte's sister, running the other. She realized that even though her passion is design, she has a way with management and bossing people around.

We are all married with kids, and we couldn't be happier.

We're headed to our home for the celebration barbecue. Connie is home cooking up a storm now, and I need to be there to help her. Even though she won't let me do a thing since I'm pregnant with our second daughter.

Boy, have we come a long way, but through it all, we have persevered, overcame, and conquered the world together.

Lamonte takes me in his arms with Dahlia on his hip, "I love you, my love, and I hope you're ready because I'm ready to start trying for our third. I need a boy around here."

"Oh really? Well, we'll see about that after this one. I already feel like I'm about to burst!" He kisses me on the lips, and still, after all these years, I feel the electricity run straight down my spine. "Um. I love you too, babe."

ALSO BY NICOLETTE JOHNSON

Don't forget to indulge in all volumes of the *Handcuffed* Series:

Handcuffed

Shackled

Bounded

Entangled

Let me know how you like the series thus far

Facebook @authornicolettejohnson

Twitter @PenNicoletteJo

Instagram @authornicolette

www.authornicolettejohnson.com

Coming Soon:

The Savannah Finest Series:

Alpha Watch